Unicorn Quest

Honey & Avery Roman

ISBN: 9798215870839

DEDICATION

For Alice, who started it all.

CONTENTS

1: The Discovery 1

2: Waking up a Unicorn 7

3: Angelina Flees.. 13

4: Running Home 21

5: The Wizard.. 25

6: A Choice 31

7: Warbel 35

8: The Berry 43

9: The Queen Eagle 49

10: The Stone 55

11: Queen Cat 63

12: The Wind 73

13: The Sun's Rays 81

14: Queen of the Dawn 89

15: The Banshee's Tears 95

16: The Banshee 101

17: The Wizard.. 111

Epilogue 121

ABOUT THE AUTHORS 123

ACKNOWLEDGMENTS

Most of the credit goes to Alice, who invented the story on a hot afternoon by the pool. But it must be said that Rhyannon and Erika helped, far more than they know.

1: THE DISCOVERY

Ten-year-old Angelina Belladonna Calliope Smith stared at her homework with weary eyes. Today was terrible from start to finish, and it wasn't over yet.

First, she hadn't been able to find her favorite hairband that morning before school. So, she'd had to make do with her second favorite, which was fine, except it wasn't, because it didn't go with her outfit, and there wasn't time to change.

On the way to the bus, she'd dropped her lunch pail and broken her thermos. Mom had lent hers, but it didn't fit in her lunch pail, so Angelina had to carry it separate, which was a pain in the neck. Literally. It put extra weight in her backpack, making her shoulders and neck hurt. Just a little, but still…

By the end of school, all her teachers had all assigned homework, which she'd been working on for the past hour.

She'd already written one essay and completed an entire page of math problems tonight, and there was still a half-page of science questions to answer before she went to bed.

She laid her head on her arms and groaned.

"I hate school, Mom."

"Do you? Or are you just tired of homework?" Her mother turned from the stove where she was stirring pasta into a pot of boiling water.

Angelina lifted her head to study her hands. "Do you think unicorns have to do homework?"

Mom gave her the side-eye. "If they go to school, yes," she said after a moment.

Angelina grinned. "I'll bet they don't."

"Oh really? Why is that?"

Angelina wiggled her fingers in the air. "No opposable thumbs. Can't do writing or science experiments or math without them, can you?"

"Maybe not, but I'd bet they have other kinds of things. Fencing practice, for one." Mom tapped the spoon on the edge of the pot, then raised it, sword-like, into the air and took up a fencing stance. *"Engarde!"*

"Mom!" Angelina rolled her eyes as she pulled her science book closer. "Unicorns don't fence. And you're dripping water on the floor."

Mom dropped a towel on the floor and shrugged as she mopped it around with her foot, drying the spots of water. "I'll bet they do. They have to use that horn for something."

"Yeah, well, I wish I was a unicorn," Angelina muttered. "At least I wouldn't have to answer a bunch of science questions every night."

"There are worse things," Mom said.

Angelina didn't ask what kind of things. She just answered the first question on the assignment and pushed the science book into her backpack with a sigh. "My brain hurts. Can I do the rest after dinner?"

Her mom looked at her. "You can, but remember it's movie night, and it's your night to choose."

Angelina brightened. "That's OK. There are only three more questions. It won't take long. Can I go play with

2

Sarah before dinner?"

"Sorry, my love, there isn't time. Dinner will be ready in about ten minutes. I need you to set the table and then call your sisters in."

"Maaaahmmmmuh! I've been doing homework all afternoon. Can't I go play for just a few minutes? Pleeeeesuh!"

Mom looked at her eldest daughter and sighed. "I'm sorry, honey, but there just isn't enough time. Please set the table and then call your sisters in."

Angelina stomped to the cupboard where the plates were and took down a stack, then slapped the first one on the table with a crack.

"Angelina."

Angelina smacked the second plate down.

"Angelina Belladonna."

Wham went the third plate. It struck the edge of the butter dish, and a little chip flew off, striking the wall with a snap.

"Angelina Belladonna Calliope Smith." Mom didn't raise her voice, but Angelina went still anyway. Whenever Mom used your full name, you knew you were in trouble. "I would like to remind you that when we break things on purpose or out of temper, we replace them with funds from our allowance."

"Yes, Ma'am," Angelina muttered. She set the rest of the plates on the table quietly. Silverware wasn't as easily broken, though, and made a satisfying clatter when she dropped a handful on the table. She stole a glance at her mother and saw that her jaw was tight. Good.

Glasses came next, then napkins, salt, pepper, bread and butter. Angelina managed it all as noisily as possible without breaking anything.

"Dinner is ready," Mom said. "Please go call your sisters."

Angelina opened her mouth as wide as it would go and

yelled for her sisters. Mom closed her eyes briefly. When she opened them again, there was a moment where Angelina thought she might have gone a step too far, but Mom only said, "From the front porch, please."

"Fine." Angelina slouched out the front door and screamed for her sisters again, even though they were less than twenty feet away, and both of them turned to look when the door opened.

All through dinner, Angelina thought about how much easier life would be if she were a unicorn. No chores. No homework. She could play all day long and not have to worry about anything. It would be the best of all possible lives.

When dinner was over, Mom popped some popcorn. "Movie night. Angelina's turn to choose."

"Woot! Princess Bride!" Angelina hooted.

"Again?" Her sister, HollyAnne's, complaint was half-hearted because she liked the movie too. Soon everyone was curled up on the couch, munching down popcorn and enjoying the improbable but highly entertaining adventures of Wesley and Buttercup.

Then it happened. Mom passed Angelina's backpack on her way in from the kitchen. "Angelina, did you finish your science questions?"

Dread pooled in the pit of Angelina's stomach. "Umm…"

"Those are due tomorrow, right?"

"Well, I…"

"Come on, you'll have to finish them before you can watch the movie with us. At least it's one you've seen before, so you aren't really missing anything."

"Can't I do the questions in the morning? Please, Mom?" Angelina loved the first part of Princess Bride when Wesley kept saying, "As you wish," and then ended up getting pushed down a hill for his troubles, and she didn't want to miss it.

"No, you can't do it in the morning," Mom said. "There won't be time."

"That's not fair." Angelina flounced into the kitchen and jerked the science book out of her backpack. The book stuck, so she tugged harder. Suddenly, it came free of the backpack like a rock from a sling. Momentum carried the volume across the table, knocking over her drink. The juice spilled all over the science homework she'd already done, ruining it.

"No!" Angelina shouted. Now she'd have to start over. This was going to take forever!

Mom grabbed a dish towel and offered to help Angelina clean up the mess.

"No," Angelina snapped. "I'll do it myself." She took the towel from Mom and mopped up the juice in wide, angry strokes, then dropped the whole, drippy mess into the trash.

"The dish towel gets rinsed out, wrung out, and put in the laundry," Mom said calmly.

"I know!" Angelina's voice was nearly a snarl, she was so mad. "If I was a unicorn, I wouldn't have to clean up this mess."

"If you were a unicorn, you wouldn't have been drinking juice," Mom said and went into the living room. Angelina wasn't sure, but she thought she caught the beginnings of a grin on Mom's face.

Anger flared through her. "This isn't funny!" she yelled at Mom's retreating back.

"I know," was all Mom said.

Angelina could hear the movie playing, and that made her even angrier. By the time she finished cleaning up the mess and answering the first question all over again, her favorite scene was over.

This was the worst night ever. All her anger drained out, leaving Angelina sad. Fat tears trailed down her cheeks as she answered the next three questions. By then, the movie was half over and it wasn't worth going into the living room to watch the rest. She went to her bedroom instead, laid down and fell asleep.

Her last thought as she stared at the canopy over her bed and her eyes drifted closed was, *I really wish I was a unicorn.*

2: WAKING UP A UNICORN

The first thing Angelina thought when she woke up the next morning was, *wow, my head feels weird.*

She tried to sit up, but her body didn't want to bend the way it usually would. Something soft and fluffy banged against her cheek. Pushing up on her arms, she tried to push it away and the hard edge of her hand scraped her skin. Startled, she jerked her hoof back and stared at it.

Angelina scrambled to stand, but she had too many legs – at least twice as many as she'd gone to bed with – and she fell off the bed, taking the covers with her onto the floor, landing in a heap.

"Errhuhuhuhu!" Angelina closed her mouth and tried to clap both hooves over it, but they wouldn't bend properly. What was that sound? Like a horse's squeal of distress, sharp and loud.

Wait. Hooves? She stared at her hands, or at what should have been hands, but there were no fingers, no thumbs. Just the hard, dark curve of… She scrambled to get up, shredding the sheets and tossing blankets everywhere.

Then her head banged against the bedpost.

Wait. No. Not her head. Something on top of her head. She tried to look up and caught a glimpse of something long and white. The fluffy thing flopped down against her face again, obscuring her vision. Suddenly, Angelina realized what it was. Her pillow. And it was stuck to her head somehow. There were feathers everywhere.

What the heck was going on?

"Angelina? What is happening? Where are you?" Mom stood in the doorway, staring at Angelina with wide eyes, but not an ounce of recognition. "And where did you get a unicorn?"

"Mom, it's me, Angelina!" Angelina tried to say, but what came out was more like, "Maaa, iyhmmee, Anheleeeeennah!" Which wasn't much help to either of them.

Mom frowned and squared her shoulders; a look Angelina knew meant business. "Who are you and what have you done with my daughter?"

Suddenly realizing that she was standing on all fours, Angelina tried to rear up and stand on her back legs. Mom's eyes got huge. Angelina's middle sister, Marianna, chose that moment to burst into the room.

"What's wrong with Angelina?" She took one look at the new Angelina and squealed with delight. "Mom! When did we get a unicorn? It's beautiful! Look at that gorgeous white coat and her mane is beautiful! Oh, my gosh! The horn! It's sparkling! Are we keeping it? What are we going to name it? I wonder if unicorns eat the same stuff as horses."

"I didn't..." Mom began faintly, as Angelina came back down on all fours.

"Ahm Anheleeeeennah!" Angelina said, trying to identify herself.

It didn't work.

Marianna peered behind Angelina. "Uhm, Mom? Where's Angelina?" Then her eyes got big. "You don't think the unicorn ATE her, do you?"

"No dear, unicorns are vegetarians."

From behind them, Angelina's youngest sister, HollyAnne, piped up. "That's Angelina, right there."

"Where?" Mom whirled around, looking frantically for her oldest child.

But HollyAnne pointed right at Angelina. "There."

Mom and Marianna followed the pointing finger, and Angelina hung her head. Everyone gasped and took a step back. Angelina realized suddenly that pointing your horn at people — even accidentally — could be considered impolite at best and threatening at worst. She raised her head.

"You think that's Angelina?" Mom asked HollyAnne.

"Of course it's Angelina," HollyAnne replied.

"How do you know?" Marianna asked.

"How can you not? Look into her eyes. That's Angelina in there, even if the rest of her looks different. Besides, she's wearing Angelina's clothes, isn't she? The ones she had on yesterday?"

Everyone stared. Even Angelina. HollyAnne was right. The seams were mostly torn, but the remnants of Angelina's favorite dress and tights were still clinging to Angelina's new body. Rather uncomfortably, now that she thought about it.

She shook herself and the tattered fabric fell on the floor.

Mom took a tentative step forward, but kept both the younger girls behind her. "Angelina?" she asked.

Angelina nodded her head up and down enthusiastically. Mom stepped back abruptly and Angelina stopped.

Mom forced a smile. "Well, at least you aren't a very big unicorn… yet. Nowhere near what you'll be full grown, I… expect. And you really are very… beautiful."

Angelina turned her head and looked at herself.

Mostly, she looked like a horse, except her tail was sleek rather than fluffy, with a cute little tuft on the end, and her hooves were more goat-like than equine. Her legs were muscular, but slender, and she had four instead of the two she was used to.

As for her face... Well, for that, she'd need a mirror, just like always. She snorted. Good to see some things hadn't changed.

Slowly, carefully, she walked out of her bedroom, discovering in the first few steps that four legs took a bit of getting used to after ten years with only two. Getting all four limbs to move in concert wasn't the simplest thing she'd ever done, but if she didn't think about it too hard, it was easier.

Her mom and sisters backed up, making room for her, then followed when she headed for the bathroom. Angelina checked the mirror first.

Her face was long and slender, with a silvery white mane hanging down the left side of her neck. Her coat was white too, and she had big, brown eyes with the longest, darkest lashes she'd ever seen.

And... No. It wasn't possible. But there it was. A little fluffy white beard dangling from her chin. If she could have blushed, she would have. Girls didn't have beards!

But the horn made up for it. Long and slender, the pure white spiral grew straight as an arrow from the center of her forehead halfway between her eyes and her ears. It was amazing, and she could have sworn it glowed, just a little, under the bathroom light.

She licked her teeth. They tasted faintly of hay, which made no sense, since she hadn't eaten anything but pasta since lunch yesterday, and she'd never eaten hay in her life.

She stared at the toothbrush with slowly dawning horror. How was she going to brush her teeth without thumbs? How was she going to eat? Get dressed? Angelina took another look at her new body. None of her clothes were going to fit.

What the heck was she going to wear?

"Maaaaaahhhhmmmmm!" she brayed, and her mom put both arms around her neck, hugging her tight as hot tears slid down Angelina's cheeks.

She was definitely going to be late for school.

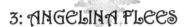

3: ANGELINA FLEES

"Unicorns don't have to wear clothes if they don't want to," HollyAnne pointed out.

"Ahma urrrllaa," Angelina said. "Nahwtaa Unnaacahwnna."

HollyAnne looked Angelina up one side and down the other. "You sure look like a unicorn.

Angelina stared at her. "Uuaa cannaa unnashanda meeaa?" she asked.

"Sure." HollyAnne shrugged. "It was hard at first, but you're getting better all the time."

"Wahl, Ahm nawt goween nahked," Angelina said.

They finally found a pair of stretchy shorts and a cute skirt with one of Mom's t-shirts for Angelina to wear. Shoes were impossible, but maybe no one would notice. The hooves were vaguely shoe-like, after all.

"Um, Angelina?" Angelina looked down and saw Marianna looking up at her. "Do you think we could have a ride to the bus stop?"

Angelina shook her head, but then wondered if the driver would even let them on the bus. Pets weren't allowed except on special days, and even then, they had to be in carriers. She had to wonder if the same rule would apply to her, now that she was a unicorn, or if she would still count as a student.

"Angelina is only nine hands high – much too young and small a unicorn to be giving rides to you two," Mom said, stepping into the bathroom while Marianna tried to measure Angelina's height with her hands. "That's about three feet, Marianna," Mom said.

She edged around Angelina's hindquarters. The bathroom was small. Two girls, a unicorn, and Mom filled it to capacity. HollyAnne climbed onto the toilet while Marianna stood in the bathtub. That helped. They would have left, but everyone still needed to brush their teeth.

Mom handed around cups, toothbrushes with the paste already on, and everyone got to work. Angeline just bared her teeth, resigned. Without fingers, brushing her own was going to be impossible.

Mom scrubbed away with the toothbrush, then stepped back. "Spit," she said.

But Angelina found that her unicorn mouth wasn't as good at spitting as her human mouth had been.

"Here," Mom said, and filled the sink with water. "Just rinse your mouth out. That will do for today. We'll figure out something better later."

Angelina followed her mom's suggestion. She was so glad to be rid of the hay taste in her teeth that she let HollyAnne climb onto her back for a ride to the living room, where mom vetoed the riding to the bus stop idea.

"HollyAnne, get off your sister. You probably aren't too heavy, but if the other kids see you riding, everyone will want to, and she really isn't big enough.

The quartet hurried out of the house to catch the bus. They rushed down the sidewalk, trying to ignore the stares of the other kids.

One boy, Rupert Finchhagle, elbowed his mom. "You said unicorns weren't real, but there one is, right there."

Mrs. Finchhagle glared at Angelina. "Hmmph. It's a costume, obviously. And it's not even Halloween. What are up to, Ms. Smith? Letting your children gallivant about in costumes during the non-costume season?"

"It's uh," Mom began, but Marianna stepped up.

"Angelina has a report on unicorns for her literature circle today. She's getting into the part."

Mrs. Finchhagle looked down the considerable length of her thin nose at the girl. "Is that so? Well, she'll have to take it off. She can't ride the bus like that. She won't fit through the doors!"

With that, Mrs. Finchhagle reached out, grabbed Angelina's ears, and pulled.

"Hey!" Mom yelled. "Let go of her!" She grabbed Mrs. Finchhagle's little finger and bent it back, not too far, just enough to make the woman release Angelina's ear. Mrs. Finchhagle howled as if she'd been ripped limb from limb.

"You attacked me! Attacker! Violent, cruel attacker!" She turned to the crowd, which was gaping at her. "You saw what she did! She attacked me!"

"What I saw," drawled Mr. Capper, the bus driver. "Was you putting hands on Angelina there."

"That isn't Angelina!" Mrs. Finchhagle shouted. "That is a unicorn!"

"But, Mom," Rupert said. "You said there was no such thing—"

"Shut up, Rupert! Don't contradict your mother!" She rounded on Angelina's mom. "What have you done with your daughter, Rosalinda Maria Smith?"

"She ain't done nothing," HollyAnne said. "That's Angelina, right there. And don't you call my mom by all her names. You aren't her mom!" HollyAnne pulled back a booted foot to kick, but Mom lifted HollyAnne into her arms, foiling the attempt.

She eyed Mrs. Finchhagle coolly. "Angelina is dressed

in costume for a presentation at school. And if you ever put your hands on any of my girls again, Darinda Elphaba Finchhagle, you will be very sorry indeed." She set HollyAnne behind her and put her hands on her hips. "Count on it."

Mrs. Finchhagle stood there with her mouth open, but no words came out.

"Get on the bus, girls," Mom said. Angelina had a little trouble with the steps, but Mr. Capper helped, and he let her take up two seats, 'just for today, so your costume doesn't get messed up,' he said.

When only Rupert was left standing on the sidewalk, Mr. Capper sat down. "You coming, Rupert?"

Rupert looked at his mom.

She looked at Angelina, then at Mom, then at Mr. Capper. "Absolutely not! You'll regret this, Rosalinda. Count. On. It." She gripped Rupert's hand and hauled him down the sidewalk, protesting all the way.

As the bus drove away, Angelina looked back and saw Mom rubbing her temples, a sure sign that trouble was coming. She just hoped she could get through the school day before it arrived.

An hour later, Angelina was more worried about being able to hold a pencil for the pop quiz her math teacher was giving than any trouble her mother might be expecting. Finally, Maria, her best friend and seat mate, taped the pencil to Angelina's hoof, solving the problem.

"I'll help you get it off when class is over," Maria whispered as Mr. Overton passed out the tests.

When Mr. Overton got to Angelina's desk, he glanced at her with concern. "Are you sure you don't want to take the head off, Angelina? Can you see the questions all right?"

"Yahs, Mahsher Ahvahtahn," Angelina said. "Awll be fahn." He nodded and Angelina sighed with relief, glad that she could make herself understood, at least. HollyAnne had been right. The more she talked, the easier it got.

She was halfway through the first problem when someone rapped on the classroom door. Angelina looked up as Mr. Overton went to answer it. Because her seat was close to the same wall as the door, and in the middle of the row, she couldn't see who was outside, but her unicorn hearing let her catch bits and pieces of their quiet conversation. Instead of sitting, she was standing, because the seat wasn't big enough for a unicorn.

Angelina's heart thudded hard in her chest, and she was suddenly glad she hadn't been able to sit at her desk like she normally would have.

"Unicorn… dangerous… custody."

"Mahria," Angelina whispered. "Ah hahv to get out ahv here."

Maria nodded and followed Angelina to the back of the class, where she opened the door to the storage room. The entire class watched in silence.

A Harry Potter poster covered a small window in the storage room door. The poster had the lower left corner torn off. Angelina had always wondered why Mr. Overton never replaced it, but when Maria put her eye to the hole, she thought maybe she knew.

"Mr. Overton let them in. He's gesturing and shrugging, like…"

"Ah cahn hear thahm. He's saying thayres naw unicahn hayre. Hay doesn't know whaht thay ahre tahking abaht."

Maria gasped. "Bobby Bristol just jumped out of his seat!" she said.

Both girls could hear Bobby yelling. "Would ya look at that! A unicorn just ran down the hall!"

Maria turned away from the door. "Both the men ran out. You gotta get home, Angelina. This is probably the only chance you're going to have."

The door opened and Mr. Overton was standing there.

17

"Angelina, come with me. Maria, well done. You are in charge of the class while I'm gone."

Maria threw her arms around Angelina's neck and hugged her goodbye, then marched to the front of the class. "Let's finish this quiz."

Mr. Overton led Angelina to the hall, looking carefully up and down it before they left the classroom. "Empty," he said. "But we need to be careful."

In a few moments, they reached the school's rear entrance. It was locked as a safety precaution, but Mr. Overton had a key. He let Angelina out through the gate. "Run home as fast as your hooves can take you, Angelina. I'll call your mother and tell her what has happened. She'll know what to do."

"Mrs. Finchhagle called them, didn't she?" Angelina asked.

Mr. Overton sighed. "I'm afraid she did, yes."

"Then this is my fault. I've brought trouble to my family and my school."

Mr. Overton's jaw clenched. "This is not your fault. You've done nothing wrong."

"I did. I made the wish, and now the military is after me."

Mr. Overton patted her shoulder kindly. "They have no right to chase you or demand anything of you, Angelina. They should know better. You have every right to be who you are, whether that's a little girl or a unicorn. Don't forget that."

Angelina sighed with relief. "Thank you, Mr. Overton. I won't forget."

From overhead came a strange, metallic thwup, thwup, thwup of something large and heavy beating against the air. Angelina looked up.

Two silver-gray helicopters with the blue and silver air force insignia on the side hovered over the school.

A booming voice shook the air. "For your own safety,

18

send out the unicorn."

Engines revved and three news vans careened around the corner, rushing up the street to the school's front entrance.

"Run. Stay under the trees as much as possible," Mr. Overton said.

He turned back toward the school, ducking under the first covered walkway as the gate clanged shut between them.

Angelina kept to the shade of the trees as he told her and ran

4: RUNNING HOME

She made it to the edge of her front yard, but once there, a gap yawned between the hedge that fenced the lawn and her front door. Angelina got down on her belly and wiggled between two of the bushes that made up the hedge, hoping the thick leaves would hide her.

It seemed to work. The helicopters circled overhead, searching for her.

But she couldn't stay here forever. What was she going to do?

Mom stepped out onto the porch, staring at the aircraft, one hand shading her eyes from the morning sun. Angelina shivered with fear. What if they hurt her mom?

"You there, the unicorn hiding in the hedge!" A man's voice thundered through the air. "Move away from the foliage and lay down on your stomach in the open grass. Obey and you will not be harmed."

Mom's eyes widened in alarm. She stared at the hedge and the color drained out of her face as Angelina's horn peeked over the leafy top. She ran down the steps toward the hedge. "Angelina!" she yelled. She fell to her knees when she reached the hedge, running her hands over Angelina's coat. "Are you hurt? What happened?"

"Mrs. Finchhagle snitched ahn me to the Air Fahrce, and they showed up at mah school!"

Mom's mouth pressed shut. When she spoke, her voice was angry and determined. "That woman has a lot to answer for. Right now, though, we need to figure out how to get you to someplace safe."

Zip-whir! The sound ripped through the air and Angelina shivered as it repeated several times. The slap of boots on asphalt followed.

"Angelina, there isn't much time. Listen carefully. When I give the signal, you run as fast as you can to the woods. They won't be able to track you there. There are a lot of magical people there, and maybe you can find help. Just..." Mom hesitated, her eyes taking on a faraway, worried look. "Just be careful who you trust. Not everyone is who they seem to be. Understand?"

Angelina didn't, really. But she knew Mom didn't have time to explain, so she nodded.

Boots crunched on the concrete sidewalk. "Ma'am, for your own safety, we need you to step away from the unicorn. They are dangerous creatures."

Mom jumped to her feet and turned around, her wild hair flying, standing out around her head like a halo. "Says who?" she snapped.

The man, a young officer, based on the insignia on his collar, stepped back. "Well, umm, all the books say so, Ma'am."

"Books can be wrong." Her hand behind her back so that only Angelina could see, Mom pointed toward the woods behind the house. Angelina inched out from under the hedge, just a couple of inches, getting ready. Mom held up three fingers. Angelina inched out a little more.

Mom stepped toward the officer. "That isn't really a unicorn. That is my daughter, in a unicorn costume. This is all a stupid mistake." She held up two fingers, still hiding them so the officer couldn't see, but Angelina could. Angelina was halfway out from under the hedge now, hoping the officer couldn't see her mom's hand.

"Now, Ma'am, that is good to hear. We can just inspect the costume and if that's true, we'll be on our way. But we have a report of an unlicensed unicorn and, according to section 42.8 of the mythological beast control code, we have to investigate. You understand." He gave her a fake smile and took a step closer.

Mom put down another finger and held her ground. Angelina was all the way out from under the hedge now, ready to spring up and run. "You are on private property, Lieutenant. If you don't have a warrant, I suggest you leave before I call the cops and my lawyer."

Angelina looked past her mom. The officer was alone. Angelina had seen Mom at the last school board meeting and knew he'd made a mistake.

The officer grinned. "Now, Ma'am, you may not realize this, but you could call out the whole Dabbletown police force and it wouldn't do you any good. I can tell you've never dealt with the U.S. Air Force before, so I'll—"

"And I can tell you've never dealt with a mother defending her child before," Mom said, and Angelina jumped to her hooves. Mom dropped the last finger and Angelina ran for the woods.

Mom tackled the officer with a scream that shook the leaves on the hedge. The officer yelped and Angelina almost looked back, but she was afraid of what she might see.

"Run, Angelina!" Mom yelled. "I'll hold him off."

No one chased her on the ground, but the helicopters didn't wait around for orders. They sped after Angelina, firing net balls at her. Brown and green puffs of earth and grass erupted from the ground on either side of her, making

Angelina's heart race in terror.

Angelina ran faster, until the ground blurred under her hooves, the grass becoming a skein of green silk dotted with smears of white that Angelina barely recognized as the little wildflowers she and her sisters liked to braid into crowns.

It seemed like one of those terrible dreams where you run and run, but your destination never gets any closer. But even the worst dreams end. The forest seemed impossibly far away one moment and the next; trees loomed over her.

The helicopters veered off, then backtracked, settling down into the open field, but by then, Angelina was in the forest, dodging trees and boulders, pushing deeper into the green darkness.

She ran as fast as she could, leaping over small streams, skipping around bushes and jumping over fallen logs, her unicorn body little more than a pale streak against the dark forest.

At first, the shouts of her pursuers followed close behind her, but with every beat of her hooves, the sounds grew fainter, until finally, they faded into silence. Still, Angelina ran on, putting as much distance between her and them as possible.

What seemed like hours later, she stumbled to a halt, leaning hard against a tree, her sides heaving, trying to catch her breath. A stream tumbled by, and she drank from it greedily, her throat dry from running so long without rest. The sun was low between the trees, setting the sky on fire with sunset reds and golds.

Angelina scanned her surroundings, and her heart sank.

She'd left her pursuers behind, and that was good, but she was also totally, completely lost.

5: THE WIZARD

As the sun set beyond the western trees, the darkness thickened. Small, unseen creatures scurried through the underbrush, making Angelina's skin bunch and creep. An owl screeched overhead, seeking prey. Angelina jumped, even though she was far too big for an owl to eat.

At least, she hoped she was.

A shadow, huge and humped with long, swinging arms, thumped between the trees to her left, trailing a stench like rotting garbage. She crouched behind a boulder until the noise and smell of it faded away. In the distance, something small and helpless screamed and Angelina shuddered.

The forest wasn't safe. She felt the danger of it in her bones. She wanted to go home. Last night's desperate wish to be a unicorn seemed stupid now. Angelina would give anything to be an ordinary girl again. She'd even do her homework without complaining.

Half-cup size tears overflowed her eyes and dripped down her broad cheeks, making the glimmer of light in the distance flare into a star.

Wait.

What was that?

Angelina peered through the dark woods, moving her head this way and that until she spotted the gleam of a single candle. She'd read enough fairytales to be wary of unexplained lights in the middle of forests, but it was dark and cold, and she was tired after all that running.

What harm could it do to at least investigate? If the people were nice, maybe they'd let her use the phone to call her mom. And if they weren't… Well, maybe there was a barn she could sleep in. No one even needed to know she was there.

She didn't let herself consider the difficulty of hiding a pony-sized unicorn, even in a barn.

Careful to keep the light in view, Angelina threaded her way between the trees, doing her best to make as little noise as possible. After what seemed like hours, but was actually closer to five minutes, she found herself on the edge of a small clearing.

In the center was a tiny, thatched cottage — little more than a hut, really. A hedge of dried sticks surrounded walls of white-painted-stone, which Angelina thought was strange. The blue paint on the front door was cracked, but the wood looked solid, and the frame of the only window matched, though it was a tad crooked. A small chimney perched unsteadily on the roof sent up a thin curl of smoke. The thin gray tendril spiraled lazily into the star-bright night sky, and there in the window was the candle.

But the cottage was all by itself. There was no village, and no barn. Something told Angelina that a house lit by candlelight wouldn't have a phone, either.

Fighting the sudden urge to run and not look back, Angelina shivered. Running away meant sleeping in the woods. Was that option any better?

Still, she was already turning around when the door flung open and a wizened old man, gray-haired, with gnarled hands and a hooked nose, stepped out onto the stoop. His dark robes were tattered at the hem and cuffs. His conical hat of matching material had a sharp bend in the middle and was covered in silver stars and moons.

"Here now! You aren't going to leave without at least offering a greeting, are you, Angelina Smith?"

Angelina froze. "How do you know my name?" she asked.

"I am a wizard." The old man chuckled. "You'll find I know a great many things. Come inside, enjoy some supper and the warmth of my fire so that I might explain."

The voice inside that told her to run before now shouted the word in her mind. Angelina shivered and took a step back.

The old man smiled gently. "I know you must be frightened. If I'd had the day you've had, I would be afraid too. But I have seen everything that has happened to you, and I believe I can help. I promise I won't hurt you."

Angelina paused. Could he really help? Did he really want to? She wished her mother was there. She'd know what to do.

"I understand your hesitation," the wizard said. "I'll tell you what. I'll leave the door open. You take all the time you need to decide. If you choose to go, I'll take no offense. But there's good food waiting. Hot soup and warm bread, plus chocolate cake for dessert. And I've a warm place by the fire for you to sleep tonight, if you choose to stay."

He said nothing more, just went back inside, leaving the door open.

The rich, yeasty scent of fresh bread drifted out to her, and Angelina's stomach growled. She'd been running all day with nothing but the few sips of water she'd managed from the streams along the way. She'd even missed lunch.

Angelina looked over her shoulder into the dark forest. A cold breeze whispered through the leaves, making her shiver. The sun was gone, and the trees hunched close. She couldn't see any stars, and the intertwined branches over her head hid the moon.

Worst of all, she didn't know where she was. It didn't seem as if she had any other choice. Angelina took a deep breath and entered the wizard's cottage.

Angelina stopped with her front hooves just inside the doorsill and let her mouth hang open. The cottage was three times larger inside than the outside had led her to believe was possible.

An enormous fireplace took up most of the east wall. A great, black cauldron hung over the flames on a hook. Inside it, a savory soup bubbled merrily. Nearby sat a long oak table, set for two with white crockery plates and silver utensils. A crusty loaf of bread steamed faintly, with a knife sticking up out of the center, and a full crock of butter next to it.

Two doors on the other two walls led to other rooms. Angelina guessed one of them was probably a bedroom and she hoped the other was a guest room. Her legs ached from running and her eyes were heavy with fatigue.

"Come in, come in. No need to let the heat out," the wizard said, though not unkindly.

Angelina stepped inside and let the door swing closed. It slammed harder than she expected, making her jump, but the wizard didn't seem to notice. He ladled soup from the cauldron into a wide, shallow bowl and set it on the table next to another, equally wide bowl.

"You'll find these easier than a cup, I'm thinking," he said.

Angelina thought this was very considerate. She walked over to the table but found a bench in the way. The wizard was watching and pulled out his wand. He pointed it at the bench and a streak of silver light zapped from the tip. As the bench shrank to the size of dollhouse furniture, he stepped forward and scooped it off the floor.

"We probably won't need this while you're here." He

smiled at her and tucked the bench into the pocket of his long sapphire blue robe. He took off his hat and hung it on a convenient hook near the fire. His white hair hung long and thick to his shoulders while his obsidian black eyes peered at her curiously.

She watched him ladle a cup of soup from the cauldron and blow on it. He sipped it, then poured each of them some water from a silver pitcher. It felt weird to eat with him watching her, but after a moment, he looked away to cut some bread for them and she drank some water and sipped carefully at the hot soup.

It was delicious.

The bread was wonderful, too.

With the worst of her hunger sated, Angelina had some questions. "You said you saw everything. How did you do that?"

The wizard leaned back in his chair to smile at her. "Excellent question. I have a crystal ball." He pointed to a round table in the corner where a six-inch globe of clear crystal sat on a carved pedestal. "I try to keep watch on the surrounding towns, just in case."

"In case of what?"

The wizard's eyes shifted. "Oh, you know, things. Honestly, you surprised me. Most accidental shifters don't learn to speak so quickly or so well as you have. You should be quite proud of yourself."

"Accidental shifters?"

"Oh yes. It happens more than one might think. Children reach a certain age and… change… suddenly."

"How does that happen?"

"Oh, any number of ways. Usually, it's the result of a malign spell cast by an enemy. Occasionally, it's a latent ability that surfaces unexpectedly." He eyed her keenly. "I believe yours is the former case."

"A malign spell? Who would want to put a spell on me?"

"You can't think of anyone who might want to cause you trouble? Make life difficult for you?"

The memory of Mrs. Finchhagle flashed through Angelina's mind, but she kept the name to herself. "I guess," she said.

"All of us have enemies, Angelina. It's nothing to be ashamed of. But very few people are as brave or resourceful as you. I keep an eye out for your kind. Try to help if I can. But most don't find their way to me, and there isn't much I can do long distance." He patted her shoulder. "I'm glad you made it here."

Angelina looked at him and sidled a step away. His hand dropped, but he kept smiling. "Why?" she asked.

"Why do I keep an eye out?"

"Yes. And why are you glad I made it here?"

"Well, I keep an eye out, because I like to help when I can, but I'm not able to go far from my cottage these days. These old bones don't let me travel as I used to. So, I watch through my crystal ball, and sometimes, I'm able to send guides or messages to those in need, to help them get here. That wasn't necessary with you, though." He chuckled and wagged a finger at her. "You were smart enough to follow the path through the forest, though it is faint, and hard to find."

Angelina blinked at him, wondering if this was what crazy looked like but too polite to ask. She'd crashed through the brush and bruised herself on stones. She'd leaped over streams and scraped past trees. There had been no path that she'd seen, and yet, here she was, so maybe she'd been following some instinct after all.

It was nice that he thought she was smart, anyway.

6: A CHOICE

"Now, the first thing we need to do is determine whether someone did, in fact, hex you," the wizard said, leaning his arms on the table.

"How do we do that?" Angelina asked warily.

He smiled encouragingly. "I have a simple test to find out."

Angelina wasn't so sure. "Will it hurt?"

"Not a bit." He turned to a shelf on the wall and chose a blue jar. Placing it carefully on the table, he pulled off the stopper and plucked a small blue stone from inside, then held it up for her to see. "This is a bezoar. Usually, they detect poison, but I've modified this one to detect hexes. That is why it is blue instead of the mucky green or brown you usually see."

Still doubtful, Angelina eyed the round, smooth stone. It didn't look dangerous, but her mother had told her to be careful. "What do I have to do?"

The wizard laughed. "Nothing at all, my dear. Just stand still." He moved closer and ran the stone over the skin above her eyes. The bezoar was warm. When he stepped back and showed the rock to her, Angelina gasped.

It glowed bright red.

The wizard looked sad and a little angry. "You have indeed been hexed, dear girl. But do not worry. We won't let the person who did this get away with it."

"We won't?" Angelina wasn't sure what he meant. And even if Mrs. Finchhagle had put a spell on her, Angelina didn't want to hurt her.

"Of course not. I believe I have a potion that will change you back."

Angelina's heart beat fast. "You do?"

"Well, I have the recipe. But sadly, I don't have the ingredients. You'll have to provide those yourself."

Angelina sighed, her heart sinking. "I don't have any ingredients."

"Of course you don't. What I meant was, you'll have to procure them for me. I'd get them myself, but as I said, my age and infirmity keep me close to home these days. You, however, are young and strong. Obtaining five easily found items will be a simple thing for you."

He said it as if he was talking about a trip to the grocery store, but Angelina noticed that he wouldn't look at her. "What items?" she asked.

He smiled. "Nothing too difficult. You'll need a red berry from the great tree, a blue gem, a bottle of wind, a ray of sunshine and the tears of a banshee."

Angelina sucked in a breath. "The berry and the stone might not be too hard, but the others? Where would I find those?"

"Oh, it won't be any trouble at all. Here is a satchel to put the ingredients in. There are a few extra containers in there for you. Probably not enough for everything, but it's a start." He laid a leather sack on the table, its long strap hanging off so she could slip it over her neck easily enough. "And I've taken the liberty of making you a list." He pulled a slip of paper from his pocket and laid it on the table next to her plate.

It said:

A red berry from the great tree atop the highest mountain.
From the deepest cave inside the tallest mountain, a sapphire
without stain,
A bottle of wind caught in the midst of its blowing
Sunshine woven from the last glimmer of its shining,
The tears of a banshee, taken as she is weeping
Gather these with courage and integrity,
Speak the spell, so that the cure of ages
Yours shall be.

Angelina slumped against the table, rattling the dishes. "The highest mountain? The deepest cave? Where am I going to find these things? Geography is my worst subject."

She paced back and forth, thinking over the rest of the list. "As for bottling the wind, or weaving sunshine — is that even possible? And don't even get me started on the tears of the banshee. All the stories say those creatures are pure evil. Even if I could get one to cry, how would I collect the tears without getting eaten?"

"You are brave and resourceful. I'm sure you'll find a way," the wizard said. "But if you can't, I'm sure life as a unicorn won't be so bad."

"Not so bad? The military chased from home me this morning. Where am I supposed to sleep?"

"Well, you can sleep here tonight. Think things over. In the morning, you can make your decision. There's an enchanted village not too far from here. If you decide to stay a unicorn, I'll take you there. I'm sure you can find work."

"Work?" Angelina said. "I don't mind chores — or not much, anyway. But I'm just a kid. I should be in school."

The wizard laughed, though not unkindly. "Dear child. Unicorns finish school by the time they are a year old, and you are far beyond that. I'm afraid you'll have to earn your keep somehow, if you choose to remain as you are." He paused to let that sink in before going on. "But do not fear. The villagers are always looking for new people — erm —

I mean to say, new inhabitants. And they aren't picky. No, not picky at all, about the, erm, species, of the immigrant."

Two fat tears rolled down Angelina's face, and the wizard looked at her with sympathy. "There now, get some rest. I'm sure everything will look better in the morning." With a flick of his wand, he produced a pillow, some blankets, and a thick, soft pallet on the floor near the fire. "I'd offer you a bed, but mine's the only one there is, and my rheumatism aches something fierce if I sleep on the floor. Price of getting old, I suppose. You understand."

Angelina nodded miserably. He patted her shoulder and blew out the candles. A moment later, he trundled off through one of the doors she'd noticed earlier. She guessed it was his bedroom.

In the flickering firelight, Angelina stared at the pallet. It didn't look uncomfortable. The opposite, really, but she missed her mom and sisters. She missed her cat and her own soft bed.

Slowly, she laid down, bending her legs gracefully at the knees and laying her head on the pillow. Using her teeth, she pulled up the blanket and made herself as comfortable as possible. Even though she was exhausted, it was a long time before she fell asleep.

7: WARBEL

Morning sun streamed through the cottage's single window, making a patchwork of bright squares on the dusty floor. The fireplace was cold with ashes, and cool air danced in the corners.

Angelina made her pallet as neat as she could without hands to fold the blankets, and slipped the satchel over her head, settling the strap across her chest, wondering all the while if there would be anything to eat.

She couldn't recall ever being quite this hungry at breakfast time before, and she wondered if unicorns got hungrier than people all the time, or if it was because of how far and fast she'd run the previous day.

The bedroom door creaked, and the wizard trudged into the living room, his hat shoved down over his tangled hair, barefoot, wearing the same wrinkled robe she'd seen him in the night before.

"Ah, you're awake! Excellent. I hope you are feeling better today!"

She wasn't, but it would do no good to say so. Instead, she said, "I've decided to try to find the ingredients." Sometime during the night, it had come to her that this was her only option. She couldn't go home, because the Air Force was probably still waiting, and she couldn't put her family in danger. Besides, she didn't know the way.

She didn't know the way to the tallest mountain either, but she'd ask the wizard about that. Surely someone as wise as he would know.

Only he didn't.

"Oh, I can't help you there," he said when she asked him. "I haven't left my cottage for a very long while. And even before that, geography was never my strong suit."

"But you're a wizard. You must know where to find these things!"

"Oh no, I'm afraid not. I can mix the potion and say the spell, you see, but finding the ingredients — no, no, that's not my job. Never been good at adventuring, myself. I've always left that to others."

Angelina eyed him sourly. "You are no help at all, are you?"

The wizard drew himself up as tall as his short stature would allow. "I have been immensely helpful. I gave you food, and lodging and a list of ingredients for the spell to reverse your curse, didn't I? Not many could have done that much. Not many would have!" He stomped out the front door, muttering about ungrateful children who didn't know their tail from a lamppost.

Shame welled up in Angelina as she followed him. Her mother had taught her to be polite and kind. "If you can't be kind," she'd always said. "Be quiet."

"I'm sorry, Mr. Wizard. You have been helpful. It's just…" She trailed off, her throat tight. "I don't know where to look for these things, and I don't want to stay a unicorn."

The wizard turned around. "That's quite all right. Perfectly understandable. Now, I'm sure if you set off through the woods and concentrate very hard, you'll figure out how to get the ingredients." He pushed at her shoulder and Angelina obliged him by turning away from the cottage.

A moment later, she heard the door slam behind her. When she looked over her shoulder, the cottage was gone, the forest clearing empty as if the hut had never been there.

Angelina blinked. Had she imagined the whole thing?

You will find me again when you have the ingredients for the potion. The words floated to Angelina like a whisper on the morning breeze and she spun around, looking for the wizard, but no one was there.

Her stomach rumbled. For someone as helpful as the wizard claimed to be, he came up short in a lot of ways. He hadn't even fed her breakfast.

Something dark and feathered flashed close to her head, and she flicked her ear, shooing whatever it was away.

"I know where you can find some breakfast," came a high, sweet voice.

Angelina tossed her mane in surprise and reared on her hind legs, looking for the speaker. A wren sat on a tree branch, watching her, but otherwise, she was alone.

"Who was that?" Angelina asked.

"It was me, silly," the voice said.

Again, Angelina whirled around, searching for the speaker. Again, she saw no one but the wren.

"Stop fooling around. Come out of hiding," Angelina said.

"I'm not hiding. I'm right here in front of you." The person giggled. "But you do look funny jumping around like that and kicking up your hooves."

"I'm not jumping around. I'm trying to see you." Angelina was a little afraid, but mostly angry. It sounded like whoever was talking was laughing at her.

"You have seen me. You just didn't know who you were looking at."

Suddenly, Angelina stopped, her gaze settling on the

wren. She stared. "Wrens don't talk," she said at last.

"Neither do unicorns, usually. But there are exceptions to almost every rule." This time, Angelina noticed that the wren's beak opened and closed in time with the words. It was talking to her!

"How… What…"

The wren ruffled her wings and hopped twice on the branch. "Come on, there's a nice berry patch just a few hundred yards from here. Might as well eat while we talk." She launched herself into the air and circled Angelina's head. "Once you regain the ability, that is. Follow me."

She flew off through the forest, zig zagging gracefully around trees and over bushes. It took Angelina a moment to recover, but then she followed at a run, the promise of berries for breakfast an opportunity not to be missed.

She didn't have to follow for long before they arrived at a small clearing. Angelina could hear a stream close by, so she knew she'd have water, but first, berries! Several bushes full of ripe blueberries grew close by the path.

"There's spinach and carrots over here too. That'll fill you up, for certain," the wren said.

Angelina wrinkled her long nose. "I don't like spinach."

The wren perched on a twig that bobbed under her weight. "Human you doesn't like spinach. I'll bet unicorn you likes it just fine. You should try it and see."

Angelina snorted and nipped a mouthful of blueberries from the bush. Maybe she would and maybe she wouldn't, but the berries were a sure thing. She'd eat them first.

"Mom always throws the carrot tops away, but I can probably dig up some of the carrots," she said.

"What!?" The wren bounced in agitation. "That's criminal! The tops are the most nutritious part!" She shook her feathers and then preened them back to smoothness. "When you get home, you need to tell her to put those into salads. You'll all be healthier for it."

Angelina frowned at her. "Sure, I will. What's your name, anyway?"

"Warbel," the bird said without hesitation. "Which item from the list will you search for first?"

Wary now, Angelina pulled another mouthful of berries from the bush. "What list?"

Warbel hopped twice, letting out a trill of laughter. "The list the wizard gave you, silly. I was watching at the window. Saw the whole thing. You'll have to do better than that if you want to fool me. Like most small creatures, I see way more than you big'uns give me credit for."

Angelina didn't say anything. She wandered over to the carrots and pawed at them, scraping two from the ground. They were dirty and scratched, but she was still hungry. She picked them up by the tops and headed for the sound of water. At least she could wash them first.

Her tongue touched the greens, surprising her with their fresh, bright flavor. Maybe Warbel was right and unicorn tastes were different from human tastes. She'd try the spinach next.

"You can trust me, you know. I'm on your side."

Startled, Angelina jumped, dropping the carrots. She looked over her shoulder to see the wren peering at her with bright eyes from a nearby branch. "I don't know you," she replied.

"Time and proximity will heal that," the bird said. "But I promise, you can."

"Which is just what someone I shouldn't trust would say."

Warbel thought that over. "Fair enough," she said after a time. "But in my case—" She stopped abruptly and leaped into the air. Flying high, she shot through the treetops and circled twice, then dropped like a stone. "Quick, hide in the brush."

"Why?"

The wren glared at her. "Because if you don't, the Air

Force will have you in a cage in less than five minutes. Hide!"

In the distance, a voice shouted and received an answer back. Angelina looked up and down the path in panic. Where was she going to hide?

"Here," Warbel said, hovering over a boulder near the stream's bank. "You'll have to go into the water but come around and there's space enough underneath. Quick!"

Another shout carried on the still air, closer now. Angelina clopped into the water, circled the boulder, and saw a mass of brush and roots on its other side. "Where... I don't see..."

"Push it away, but don't let go. You'll need to pull it back for cover!"

Angelina nudged at the sodden brush with her hoof, gasping in shock when it floated away from the boulder. Nudging the brush aside revealed a hollowed-out area under the stone big enough for her to hide in. The water was knee deep, not a space she'd want to sleep in, but if she pulled the deadfall in after her, no one would ever know she was there.

A shout from the clearing made her heart hammer, and she hustled into the little cave, pulling the tangle of branches and debris close behind her.

"Good," Warbel said softly. "Now, don't come out until I say. Stay hidden."

Angelina didn't have time to answer. With a flutter of wings, Warbel was gone. A minute later, Angelina heard a voice remarkably like her own shout, "Silly Air Force folks! You can't catch me!"

A trill of laughter that was all Warbel echoed through the trees and men shouted, "There she goes, get her!" The crash and crunch of humans chasing something through the forest filled the air, then faded, but Angelina didn't move.

The chilly water lapped around her knees, growing colder by the minute. Soon, her skin was numb, and her joints ached. It wasn't bad, yet, but she knew the longer she stayed, the worse it would get, especially since there wasn't much room to move in the small cave.

Had she been a girl, she could easily have climbed up on the narrow sandbar at the cave's rear, but as it was, that space wasn't big enough even for a young unicorn.

She shivered, her horn brushing irritatingly against the rocky ceiling, and she'd just decided to wait five more minutes before leaving the cave, when a whistle sounded outside.

"Unicorn? Are you still inside? You didn't drown, did you? Because that would ruin everything."

Angelina nudged the tangle of roots aside and trudged out of the cave. "My name is Angelina. Are you sure it's safe? And what do you mean, it would ruin everything?"

"Pleased to meet you, Angelina. Yes, it's safe. Those Air Force folks will chase their tail feathers all the way to Dabbletown before they realize a bird tricked them."

"And the last bit?" Angelina climbed onto the riverbank and picked up the carrots she'd dropped. She was still hungry.

"Oh, that. Well, it turns out that the wizard took something from me a long time ago, and I'm hoping that, once I've helped you become human again, you'll help me get it back."

Warbel perched on a branch and looked upstream, away from Angelina, as she spoke. Angelina dipped the carrots in the water and swished them around, then dropped them in a patch of clean grass. "He stole from you?"

The bird hopped twice on the branch. "He took something that belonged to my family. No one was home to tell him no. But the fact is, what he took was mine, and I want it back."

Angelina munched on a carrot, trying some greens with it and finding them surprisingly tasty. She swallowed. "How will you help me?"

"I know where to find all the ingredients. I can't get them for you, but I can help you find them, and I know some things that will help you get them without getting killed along the way. Do we have a deal?"

Angelina crunched another carrot. She thought about how the wren had risked herself to lead the soldiers away. Asking the wizard to give back something that didn't belong to him in the first place didn't seem like a lot for the bird to ask in return for her help.

She lifted her head and looked at Warbel sitting on the branch above her.

"We have a deal."

8: THE BERRY

Angelina followed Warbel through the forest. At first, the path was easy; wide and level, with few turns to make the going difficult.

But soon enough the trail rose, trending uphill, and the land grew rocky, the vegetation sparse. Warbel perched in a tall oak on a riverbank. "Better drink here. It will be your last chance for a while."

She took the bird's advice and drank deeply. "Now what?"

Warbel ruffled her wings. "Now we cross."

Angelina looked at the water. The river was thirty yards across here. Some of it looked calm enough, but there were also wide swathes of swift current and bubbling white water curling around jagged rocks and fallen logs. Pretty to picnic beside, but not a swimmer's paradise.

"You're kidding, right?"

"I wish I was, but the closest bridges are three days' travel in either direction," Warbel said. "Ogres guard both of them, which I don't think you're ready for. Here, the river is shallow most of the way. Follow my directions and you won't even have to swim."

The unicorn stared doubtfully at the river. None of it looked shallow. The calm parts looked deep enough to swallow her whole, and the frothy bits looked violent enough to beat her to death against the rocks. There had to be a better way across.

"I can run pretty fast. Maybe one of the bridges would be easier?"

"You've forgotten the ogres. I heard that unicorn steak is a favorite of theirs. But sure, we can try to get past them if you want."

"I thought ogres could only hunt during the night. All the stories say they turn to stone if they let sunlight hit them," Angelina said.

"It's trolls you're thinking of. Ogres do fine in the sun, though I'll admit, they like the dark better for hunting. That much is true."

"Oh." Angelina didn't know what to say to that. Fighting an ogre did not seem to be a good way to spend an afternoon, though, so she took Warbel's advice. "All right. We'll cross here then, if you think that's best."

"Wise choice. Now listen, I know the way across, but rivers are changeable, so watch your step as you follow. It shouldn't get much more than chest deep, but you never know."

Angelina's belly tightened with nerves. "Are you sure about this?" she asked.

"Not really, but we don't have many other options." Warbel flitted out over the water. With a few wingbeats, he was across the river and back again. "It looks the same. Follow me."

Angelina stepped into the river and sucked in a shocked breath as the icy water curled around her fetlocks. But Warbel was right, it wasn't deep. The unicorn moved out with more confidence, place her hooves carefully as the little stones on the river bottom tended to roll under them.

"Easy does it. I know it's cold, but take your time." Warbel flitted overhead, looped back and zoomed close to the surface, checking the depth as best she could, and leading Angelina around darker patches that hinted at deeper water.

"Screeee." The call echoed through the trees, bouncing off the water to shiver its way along Angelina's spine.

A flash of brown feathers tore through the air, sending Warbel tumbling toward the river.

"Warbel!" Angelina cried. Surging through the water, she reached the stunned little bird before she could sink. The girl inside the unicorn had never wished more for hands. She dipped into the frigid water, putting her shoulder under the wren and raising up to lift her out. "Are you all right?" she asked.

"Hawk," Warbel sputtered. "Leave me. He'll be back."

Indignant, Angelina stomped her hoof, though the effect was ruined since it was under water, dampening both the view and the sound. "I will not leave you!"

"Scree!" the hawk screamed again. Angelina looked up to see it circling for another attack.

"Quick, climb into my mane. I'll make a run for it."

"You can't. There are three pits ahead. Fall into one and you'll probably drown."

"I won't. Mom taught us all to swim when we were tiny. I'll be fine. Now, hold on."

"This isn't the local public pool!" Warbel protested, but she was already winding herself up in Angelina's mane, her tiny claws clinging to the long, damp strands.

Angelina struck out as fast as her hooves could wade. The hawk screeched overhead, and the unicorn glanced up. A loose stone turned under her hoof, and she stumbled sideways toward dark water.

"That's too deep, Angelina! Go the other way!" Warbel cried. But it was too late. The loose riverbed slipped out from under her churning hooves and Angelina slid toward the deep water.

Scrambling, Angelina regained her balance, but now the water was up to her neck. "Warbel, are you all right?"

A choking cough rasped in her right ear. "Dandy. I told you there were pits ahead."

"One down, two to go." Angelina tried to joke, but her heart was beating fast. That had been close.

"Tell you what," Warbel said. "I'll watch out for the hawk; you watch out for the pits."

"Deal," Angelina said, and slogged toward the shallower water. Overhead, the hawk screamed again, but the unicorn kept her eyes on the water, carefully avoiding the next pit of deep water.

"We're almost there, Warbel." Angelina heard the hawk and risked a quick look up. It was diving!

She ran, veering right to avoid the final pit, her hooves splashing through the shallow water. Huge wings beat against her neck, and she heard Warbel's shrill cry next to her ear. Angelina spun around, smacking the hawk with her neck and sending it tumbling through the air.

The water under her hooves was only an inch deep now. She pawed it angrily, raking the pebbles into straight rows. "Leave my friend alone," she warned.

The hawk righted itself, flapping to gain height and then plunged toward her, its talons reaching for Warbel.

Angelina lowered her horn, and the hawk back flapped, veering off at the last second. He landed on a nearby branch to glare at them.

"I said, leave her alone." Angelina stood tall and proud, her horn glinting in the sun.

The hawk preened his feathers, glancing at Angelina and Warbel every few seconds. Angelina guessed it was to see if they were still watching him. Finally, he launched himself out of the tree and flew away, but Angelina didn't trust him not to come back.

"Stay where you are for a while, Warbel," she said. "I

don't want you to be that hawk's lunch."

"Not something I was looking forward to either," Warbel replied, and perched on top of Angelina's head, right next to her horn.

After that, the trail twisted like the back of a snake, splitting around boulders and threading along narrow ledges that circled the face of the mountain. Once, it dropped off a sheer cliff face, and they had to backtrack, taking the steeper path they'd decided against before because it looked too difficult. No matter what, the path always trended upward.

Warbel was so light that carrying her was like carrying air, and Angelina didn't mind. But the path was long and treacherous. Several times, Angelina scraped her legs on boulders and cracked her hooves against rocks. By the time they reached a cave near the top of the mountain, both she and Warbel were exhausted. But the air was cool and the sky a deep, cobalt blue. Stars shone down, coating everything in their benevolent silver light.

"Is this where the berries grow?" Angelina asked.

"No. The Great Tree grows at the very top of the mountain, and there's one other thing the list doesn't mention," Warbel said.

Something in the wren's tone sent a shiver rushing along Angelina's spine. "What?" she asked softly.

"The tree grows in the garden of the Eagle Queen. You'll have to get past her to gather the berries. And she doesn't like visitors."

Angelina sighed. "Fantastic."

9: THE QUEEN EAGLE

They slept in the cave that night, and when Angelina woke the next morning, everything hurt. Her legs hurt from climbing. Her hooves hurt from smacking against stones. Her neck hurt where she'd slammed against the hawk. Her head hurt from… She didn't know why her head hurt, but it did.

"Yesterday was hard," Warbel said. "Today will be harder. Go out to the mouth of the cave and find the places where dew has gathered in the rocks. Drink and you will feel better."

"Rock water? Yuck!" Angelina yelped, horrified. Mom didn't let them eat things that had fallen on the floor in the kitchen, let alone outside on the ground. She wasn't drinking rock water.

"Morning dew in the mountains is probably cleaner than tap water from your kitchen sink." Warbel made a funny clucking sound that it took her a moment to recognize as laughter. "You are more unicorn than girl, right now. Best take advantage of it while you can."

Thirstier than she'd ever been in her life, Angelina trudged to the mouth of the cave. Craggy, gray rocks guarded the entrance, each dip and cranny filled with dew that would dry as soon as the sun rose.

She sniffed the crystal-clear water. It didn't smell bad. She stuck out the tip of her tongue and tasted one of the tiny pools.

The water was delicious! As she lapped it up, she heard a tapping from nearby. The wren was cracking open a seed pod against the rock. The shell split and a seed tumbled to into the water with a splash.

Warbel fished it out and gobbled the seed down. Angelina's stomach rumbled, and she wished she could find breakfast so easily.

She slurped up some more water instead. "Now what do we do?" she asked Warbel.

"Now, you follow that path to the top of the mountain. There you'll find the garden of the Eagle Queen."

"Me? What about you?"

"I will be waiting for you right here, if… I mean when, you get back."

"What do you mean 'if'?" Alarm zipped through Angelina's chest like lightning. "Is the Eagle Queen violent?"

"Only if you try to steal from her," Warbel said casually as she picked up another seed and cracked it against the rock.

Shocked, Angelina started, her front hooves lifting off the ground. "I'm not a thief."

"You shouldn't have a problem then. Just don't forget to bow. Eagles are sticklers for protocol."

"Protocol?"

"Rules, routines, procedures, you know. Better hurry. She'll be off to hunt breakfast soon, and who knows when she'll get back."

Angelina glared at the wren, but she just cracked and ate another seed. Giving a huff of irritation, Angelina picked her way up the narrow path that wound up the mountain peak.

It didn't take long to reach the crest and Angelina stood atop the tallest mountain looking at the world laid out before her like one of her grandmother's quilts. Patches of green and brown with long strips of blue and gold spread out from the mountain's base. She recognized the darker patches with their white and green dots as towns, and the deep green, oddly shaped bits as forests. From this height, she could even see the fluffy white puffs of clouds hiding great swathes of the world below.

Angelina shivered. Everything looked so far away.

"It is one of my favorite views, but it makes one feel very removed and lonely." The voice was crisp, and cracked with age, but it held humor and kindness around the edges.

Angelina turned slowly.

Laid out before her was an expansive garden. There were plants she recognized — strawberries and carrots, apple trees and primroses — but there were others she didn't. Vines with oddly shaped leaves and odder fruits. Bushes with tiny white berries and heavy headed flowers shaped like skulls. There were roses and gardenias and clumps of lavender and sage, but the most magnificent plant of all stood in the center of the garden.

The Great Tree was enormous. Its trunk was golden brown, the leaves every color Angelina had ever imagined, and a few that she'd never even thought of. But the fruit — the tree grew every kind of fruit in existence. Apples, oranges, plums, and peaches. Bananas, pineapples, pears, and nectarines. Then there were those that Angelina didn't recognize. Some shaped like stars or moons, others in the shape of hands. There were tiny berries in every color and huge head shaped fruits that weighed the branches they grew on down to the ground.

"It is customary, when one meets a queen, to introduce yourself." This time there was irritation in the voice and

Angelina's attention snapped back to the speaker. A huge eagle sat in the tree; her talons wrapped around the largest branch. Her feathers were brown except on her head where they were cloud white, and smooth as water flowing in a brook with no stones.

Her beak was sharp and hooked, ready to tear, but for now, she spoke. "I am Regna Aquila, queen of all the avians. This is my garden. Will you do me the honor of sharing your name and story?"

Remembering Warbel's advice, Angelina bowed deep. Something about the eagle made Angelina's voice shake as she answered. "I a-a-am Angelina Smith," she said, and the queen of the eagles inclined her head.

"I am pleased to meet you, Angelina. And what is your story?"

So, Angelina told her all that had happened in the last… Had it really only been two days? She couldn't believe it, but it had. When she got to the end, she said, "and so, your majesty, I've come to ask you for a favor. I need some red berries from the Great Tree so that I can turn back into a girl."

"I am moved by your story, child. But I must ask, why do you wish to return to your human body? Are you not still you, inside the unicorn's lovely form? And is not the unicorn's body stronger, faster, and more durable than the poor, weak human one?"

"Well, I, um…"

"Tell me, would you have made it up the mountain as a human?"

Angelina thought about it. "A lot of humans climb mountains."

"Do they? Not this mountain, I can assure you."

"It is true that my unicorn body is both strong and fast. And it can go farther than my human body could, I'm sure. But I'd still like to be a girl again."

"Why?"

"Because my family is human. And all — well, most of my friends are human. And there are things a human body can do that a unicorn body can't."

"Such as?" Regna Aquila asked sternly, and Angelina knew she was losing her chance of getting the red berries. She had to answer well and quickly.

She thought hard, and then she knew. "A unicorn's hooves are strong and swift, but they cannot scoop a friend from a rushing river, or shield that friend from a hawk's talons. They cannot write the story of a battle or a life. But human hands can do these things and much more. That is one reason I'd like to be human again, to write down the tale of my adventures."

Regna Aquila shifted her feathers and settled back on her branch. "Well said, young Angelina. You may take your berries. You'll find a box at the base of my tree to contain them and keep them from bruising. You are welcome to it. The previous owner will not be needing it any longer."

Angelina picked her way to the trunk of the Great Tree, careful not to step on any plants, and found the box as the queen eagle said she would. As she picked it up, she glimpsed something in the grass, bone-white, rod-shaped and slender. She snorted, bobbing her head up in surprise. But when she looked again, nothing was there. Setting the box down nearby, she opened the flap of her satchel with her teeth.

A raven flew to her, bringing the berries, ruby red and succulent. He dropped them into the box, tapped it shut and dropped it into her pack. Angelina nodded her thanks and let the flap go.

"Be careful of those berries," Regna Aquila said. "They are life-fruit, but they only heal the body, not the mind or soul. Eat one and any physical ailment you have will be healed. Eat two and your body will remain young, but your mind will not stop aging. Eat three, and your body will live forever, even after your soul has long since passed on."

Tilting her head, Angelina sighed. "I don't think I understand."

The queen nodded. "People say they want to live forever, but they do not consider the consequences of a mind that has grown tired of living, trapped in a body that cannot die."

Angelina took a deep breath. "Thank you for the warning, great queen. But the berries are not for me to eat. They are for the wizard who will use them in the potion to make me human again."

"Oh yes. You mentioned the wizard, but not his name."

Angelina tried to frown, but couldn't, so she shook her mane instead. "That's because… I don't know it."

"And do you trust this wizard, whose name you do not know?"

"Of course I do. He's helping me."

"Is he?" The eagle tilted her head to the side, gazing at the unicorn intently. "Why?" she asked, and before Angelina could answer, she spread her great wings and leaped into the sky.

Before Angelina could blink, the eagle was gone. Wide-eyed, the girl-turned-unicorn gazed into the empty sky. The sun was already setting. Where had the time gone?

Slowly, carefully in the gathering dark, she made her way back to the cave where Warbel waited.

"I was getting worried," the wren said. "Did everything go all right? Did you get the berries?"

Angelina nodded and curled up on the ground, resting her head on her forelegs. In a moment, she was asleep. Warbel watched for a moment before tucking her head under her wing and following Angelina's example.

10: THE STONE

When Warbel woke the next morning, the cave was empty, but an odd snuffling was drifting in from outside. She flitted toward sound and lit on a boulder next to Angelina.

The unicorn was sitting next to the cave entrance, watching the sunrise, with tears streaming down her cheeks.

"Why are we crying with such a lovely sunrise to watch?" the wren asked.

"Because getting the berries was nearly impossible, and I had you to guide me. Now I have to find a blue gemstone in the deepest cave, and I don't know where to start. What am I going to do?"

The little wren rocked back and forth on her perch, making that funny sound again.

"Why are you laughing at me?" Angelina demanded.

"What did the list say?"

"You know what it said as well as I do."

"Just repeat the first two lines."

"Fine," Angelina huffed. "Something about a red berry from the great tree—"

"Which grows 'atop the highest mountain.'"

"Yeah, yeah, and a sapphire from the deepest cave."

"Which you will find 'inside the tallest mountain.'" Warbel looked at Angelina expectantly. When she just looked at her, Warble fluttered impatiently. "What do the highest mountain and the tallest mountain probably have in common?"

Angelina snorted and tossed her mane. "It can't be that simple."

"And yet, it is." Warbel leaped into the air, flying out past the ledge where they sat and looked down at the foot of the mountain. "When you think about it, it makes perfect sense that the deepest and the highest parts of a mountain are connected. The cave you seek is at the foot of this very mountain. All you need to do is go to the bottom, and then keep going down."

Angelina peered over the edge and swallowed down the sudden lump in her throat. Her legs were still covered in bruises and cuts from the trek up the mountain. Her neck still ached a bit from where she'd slammed into the hawk. All she really wanted was a bath and one of her mother's cupcakes.

And maybe a good book and her favorite cuddly blanket to curl up in.

She shook the longings out of her head. She'd probably just get her pillow stuck on her horn again, anyway. She sighed. "All right then. Might as well get moving."

Warbel led the way, and they started down the mountain.

The second time the path ended at a cliff edge, and she had to scramble down the rocky screed like an antelope, Angelina was ready to quit. "Going down is harder than going up," she panted. "And going up was the hardest thing I've ever done."

"Life tends to be that way. Each hard thing feels worse than the last. And maybe it is, but usually it isn't."

Angelina narrowly avoided breaking an ankle on a rolling stone and turned to the wren with a quizzical expression. "What do you mean?"

"Well, whatever we're going through at the moment often seems like the worst thing that's ever happened. But half of that is the fault of hindsight, which is not 20/20, you know. More like 20/60 with rose tinting on the lens," Warbel replied.

"I don't know about that," Angelina said after thinking about it. "I have a pretty good memory."

"Of course. And you probably remember the basic facts of an event pretty well. But the level of difficulty? That's what they call subjective."

"Meaning…?"

"Meaning that it's mostly based on how you felt about it. While you were going through whatever it was, it felt challenging, maybe even impossible. But after you survived it, it doesn't seem so bad, and the further you get from the event, the less dangerous and difficult it feels. That's why you can laugh about truly awful things that happened in the past. After a while, your relief at having survived makes them seem less frightening than you thought they were at the time."

"That doesn't make any sense."

Warbel made his little-bird-laughing sound. "Humans don't make much sense."

"Do birds do that too? Remember things as less dangerous than they were?"

The wren didn't look at her but flew straight beside Angelina. "No. Birds remember everything, exactly as it happened. Forever."

"You sound angry," Angelina said. "Or sad."

"Sometimes that's the same thing," the wren replied. "Listen, you won't need me for this next bit. Be careful, listen to good advice. I'll see you when you come out."

"But—"

But Warbel wasn't there. She soared high into the leaves, disappearing from sight. Startled, Angelina stopped suddenly, and a bunch of pebbles scattered under her hooves. She'd reached the bottom of the mountain.

The trail wound left through the tree-covered hills. A stream bubbled nearby, and Angelina took a deep, grateful drink before splashing through it and following the path on the other side. Warbel didn't return, but within an hour, Angelina could tell she'd found the cave.

The mouth yawned high overhead, lined in jagged, tooth-shaped rocks; the floor was rough and red. Thick vines covered in black berries and dark green leaves grew on both sides of the cave. But Angelina wasn't tempted to taste them. Between the leaves, thorns grew, each one as long and thick as her thumb when she was human, needle sharp and shining with a liquid she was sure was poison.

Gritting her teeth, Angelina stepped inside with her front feet, leaving her rear hooves in the safe outside. Light pushed in with her, but it was as if the sunshine met a wall less than two feet from the entrance. Beyond that, the dark was so thick she could almost touch it.

Where was Warbel? For all Angelina knew, this wasn't even the right cave. She could be walking into the lair of some great, ugly, unicorn eating beast and she'd never know it.

But deep inside, she knew that this was the right place. She didn't know how, but the conviction was there, right behind her breastbone, and it wasn't going anywhere.

So, she took another step, bringing one rear hoof inside the cave. The darkness gathered closer, and she heard a sigh from somewhere deep inside the cave.

As she brought her fourth hoof inside, the light went out, leaving her in darkness, and Angelina shivered all over, her coat rippling in distress. She looked down and couldn't see her feet.

Something skittered over the rock in the dark and

Angelina jerked. In a flash, she was outside again, her sides heaving, head bobbing as she sucked in lungfuls of air.

She hadn't needed a night light since she was three, but this dark was unlike anything she'd ever experienced. Deeper, blacker, as if it had taken all the light and just… swallowed it whole.

She couldn't go back in there.

"Warbel!" Angelina shouted. "Where are you? I need your help."

Quiet pressed in on her. The woods were an orchestra of sound. Birds sang, squirrels chittered, animals scurried through the brush. The wind bustled in the leaves, and in the distance, the brook gossiped of all it had seen on its long travels, but none of these sounds were the one Angelina needed.

Warbel's voice.

Keeping the cave entrance in sight, Angelina searched the area nearby for food and found some berry bushes and several patches of wild oats and roots. It didn't take long to fill her belly. It took even less time to realize how tired she was.

She decided to lay down in a shady patch of grass to wait for Warbel to return. Or her own courage to show up, whichever came first.

Sunshine warmed her back and a soft breeze played in the tufts of hair around her ears and chin. Soon, her eyelids drooped, and her tail swished gently in the flower-strewn grass.

It felt like a few minutes later, but the long shadows suggested hours, when something skittered past her nose, huffing and puffing with exertion.

Angelina kept her body still, but couldn't stop her eyes from flying open. At the cave mouth, a mouse paused, set down the basket he was carrying and combed his whiskers with his paws. The basket was as big as the mouse's head, stuffed with packages and bundles of every shaped and size, mounded up twice as high as the wicker was deep. Angelina wondered how the mouse carried it.

The little rodent finished cleaning his face and ears, straightened his whiskers and groomed his tail. He scampered to the vines and plucked a thorn and a berry. Skewering the berry on the thorn, he tucked it into the basket with the berry poking out the front.

Then he squared his shoulders and hoisted the basket into the harness he was wearing. Angelina hadn't noticed it before because it was the same color as the mouse's fur. Pale gray and white.

The mouse took a step toward the cave and Angelina clambered to her hooves. "Wait, aren't you afraid?"

Startled, the mouse whirled around, the weight of the basket pulling him off balance. Angelina reached out and steadied him with a carefully placed hoof, but the mouse wasn't impressed.

"Here now, whatcha doin' startlin' a body like that," he squeaked. "Sneaky thing, and such a great big one, too!"

"Oh, I am sorry. I didn't mean to scare you."

"Scare me? You? Don't be daft! You didn't SCARE me!" The mouse brushed down the fur on his chest and puffed up a bit. "No one, big or small, scares Valus Mouse, and you can take that to the cheese factory. Thank you VERY much."

He eyed her carefully, and when he saw Angelina didn't mean to attack, he checked over his basket, ensuring that each package and parcel was secure and that the berry skewer remained intact.

"Gotta head in now. Don't want to be late with my deliver for the Queen." Balancing the basket, he turned and headed for the cave.

"Wait," Angelina said. "It's terribly dark in there. Aren't you afraid?"

He gave a huff of annoyance. "Afraid of what? There is nothing in the dark but more dark, and the smallest bit of light can fix that."

With that, he flicked the berry with his tail. The black fruit quivered and cracked; streaks of light shone through, lighting the way in front of him.

"How did you do that?" The question burst out of Angelina like it was on springs.

The mouse eyed her carefully. "Liquid on the thorns reacts with the berry juice, makes a bit of light," he explained.

"So, it isn't poison!" Angelina said.

"What fool told you it was?" Valus exclaimed.

Angelina didn't answer. Instead, she said, "I wish I could make one of those."

"Then why don't you?" Valus asked.

Angelina held up a hoof. "No fingers, no toes," she said.

"I see. And why do you want to go in?"

Angelina told him her story, making it brief, as he seemed impatient.

When she finished, he rubbed his tiny chin. "Oh, well. We can't let things like that stop us, can we?" He scurried to the vine and plucked a few thorns, skewered several berries, and formed them into a small ring. "Bend down now. Don't fear. I won't hurt you."

Angelina did as he asked, having to go down on both front knees so he could reach her horn. He slipped the berry circlet around her horn and tapped it sharply with his tail. The glow was so bright, Angelina had to squint.

"It'll only last an hour, so don't dawdle," Valus warned, and without another word, he ran for the entrance, stopping just at the edge. "One last thing. Seek the queen and tell the truth. Do not steal, no matter the temptation or whether you feel you've a right. The queen doesn't take thievery lightly, and she is far more powerful than she looks."

Without waiting for a reply, he scampered away into

the cave, a white glow in the dark.

11: QUEEN CAT

Angelina entered the cave and this time, though she couldn't see far, she could see the path a foot or two in front of her. It was still black dark beyond the ring of light cast by the berries, but she stiffened her spine and moved forward.

"I'll never have more courage than I do right now," she thought. "And if I don't move forward, I'll never find the stone, and I'll be stuck as a unicorn the rest of my life. I wonder how long unicorns live."

Something skittered in the darkness to her left, and she jumped, but when she turned her light that way, she didn't see anything, so she kept moving. The path wended downward, curving and turning as it went. The walls were damp, and in places rivulets of water ran down from the ceiling, forming puddles on the floor. The hall she traveled narrowed and widened with each turn, making some parts so big she couldn't see the walls, while other spots were barely wide enough for her to get through.

The journey went on for what felt like hours, though her berry ring didn't go out, and there was no way to count the passage of time in the cave. She just kept walking, going deeper and deeper into the earth.

As she walked, she wondered how she'd be able to pick up the jewel if she found it. She might be able to pick it up with her lips. They were wonderfully flexible, but she worried that the edges of the gem might be too sharp and would cut her mouth.

Perhaps her tail? But no, that wouldn't work. How would she grip the thing? Her tail had a lovely tuft of hair at the end, but that was hardly the same as fingers.

Her thoughts were so centered on these concerns that she almost didn't notice the door on her right.

She was several steps past it before she even realized it was there. The corridor was quite steep, and too narrow for her to turn. Angelina's heart pounded. What was she going to do?

She had two choices. Keep going and hope for a wider space, or back up. She took a step forward and felt the walls press against her sides. Her long unicorn body couldn't turn around, and the more she struggled, the tighter the rock walls wedged her in. She had to back up.

She pulled back. The stone scraped against her coat, pulling at the hair, catching on her satchel, but she couldn't move. She was stuck!

"No," she panted. "I can't be trapped here!"

She tried harder, putting her full weight into the effort, pushing backward with all four hooves against the stone floor. It worked. She moved an inch. Not much, but enough to let her know she could make it. She pushed again, twisting against the rock walls, and felt them scratch her sides. One more tug and she was free, stumbling backward to land on her rump, her pack smacking against her chest.

She pulled harder, putting her full weight behind it, pushing with all four hooves against the stone floor. It worked. She moved an inch. Not much, but enough to let her know she could make it. She pulled again, twisting against the rock walls, and felt them scratch her sides. One more tug and she was free, stumbling backward to land on her rump, her pack smacking against her chest.

She sat there on the cold, wet floor for a moment, catching her breath. Finally, she stood. The door was till there and she pushed it open.

The room beyond was big — the size of her entire house at home. Two brick fireplaces, one on either side, held blazing fires. Cabinets, bookcases, display racks, tables, and shelves of every kind took up the entire space. And the treasure they held!

Ornately bound books trimmed in gold and silver, jeweled cups, necklaces and earrings, richly woven tapestries and rugs hung on racks, silverware carved with insignias of royal houses, China and glassware studded with gemstones of incalculable worth. It was a treasure room to end all treasure rooms.

For a moment, Angelina just stood there, blinking.

"It's quite all right. It takes most people a moment to adjust, you know." The voice was deep and feminine and filled with power. Angelina turned her startled gaze to the fireplace on the left, where a huge, thickly padded chair stood. A petite cat sat in the chair, just as a grandmother might sit with her embroidery, a mob cap on her head, a hoop between her paws, stitching away. Her tortoiseshell fur gleamed in the firelight, and she wore a tiny, golden crown between her ears. She did not wear a collar or tags. Instead, a delicate lace and pearl necklace, three inches wide and intricately beaded, graced her neck.

Angelina could tell right away that this was no one's pet.

The sampler she was working on read 'Greed is Only the Fear of Not Having E...' The E was only half done, but Angelina could still tell what it was. She wondered what the rest of the word was going to be.

She also wondered how the cat managed to embroidery so beautifully without opposable thumbs but thought it would be rude to ask.

Perhaps she used magic.

"Come," the cat said. "Sit next to me and tell me your tale. I get so few visitors here. It is always lovely to have news of the outside." The cat tugged on the bellpull next to her chair and a faint chime sounded. A little door opened next to the fireplace and Valus popped out.

"Yes, missus?" he squeaked.

"There will be a guest for tea, as you thought, Valus," the cat said. "Will you tell Cook?"

Valus gave Angelina a quick grin. "Already done, Missus. I knew she'd make it."

The cat purred. "Very good, Valus. You are on top of things, as usual."

Valus bowed. "Thank you, Missus." He disappeared back through the door, and it swung closed behind him.

The cat turned back to Angelina. "You aren't sitting," she observed. "But I can see that the chair is not suited to a unicorn's physique. I apologize."

"Oh, no, that's quite—"

The cat twitched her tail, and the chair disappeared. In its place was a huge, round pouf, well-stuffed and covered in velvet. "There, that should work."

Angelina laid down on the pouf and found it indescribably comfortable. "This is amazing," she told the cat. "Thank you."

The cat inclined her head regally. "My name is Queen Felicity. You may call me Your Majesty or Ma'am, as pleases you."

"Oh, I, um, thank you," Angelina said lamely. "My name is Angelina Smith."

"And why are you here, Angelina Smith?"

Angelina had told her story so many times by now that she had it by heart. She finished the tale by saying, "I don't know where Warbel has gone off too, or why she left so suddenly. I hope she's all right."

The feline nodded wisely. "The wren dared not enter my castle."

"Why not?" Angelina asked.

"Oh, that is a long and delicate tale. If you ever return to this place, perhaps I will tell it to you, but for now, we should talk of other things." Felicity showed a toothy grin that made Angelina shiver, the questions she wanted to ask dying on her tongue.

And so, Felicity asked about Angelina's home and family as well as her adventures since leaving them. She was especially keen to learn more about Angelina's impressions of the Eagle Queen.

"She was very generous. She gave me the berries without asking anything in return," Angelina said.

"Did she? But you said she asked many questions, just as I have."

"Well, yes. But a few questions aren't much."

The cat's eyes glittered, and she put her embroidery down, the letters E-n-o showing brightly against the fabric. "You are mistaken, unicorn girl. Information is never nothing. What one knows or doesn't know can be the difference between living and dying." She leaned back and put another stitch into the design. "Now, I have a question for you. Why do humans worry so much?"

Angelina tilted her head, surprised. "I guess because they want things to happen, and they get concerned they won't. Or they don't want a thing to happen, and they feel, you know, worried, that it will?"

Felicity snuffled. "This is the way of the world. We can take steps to influence the course of events, but things will happen or not happen as the universe wills. It is the worrying that puzzles me."

"I think it's just part of being human," Angelina said slowly. "We worry, even though there's nothing we can really do about it."

Felicity sniffed. "And do unicorns worry?"

Angelina thought about it. The truth was, since becoming a unicorn, she hadn't had much time to worry. And the one time she had, it had almost gotten her permanently stuck. "Not much," she said at last.

"Neither do cats. And let me assure you, we are much happier animals for it. Are you sure you want to return to your human form?"

"I want to be with my family. It would be hard to live in the human world as a unicorn."

"Hard does not always mean bad," the cat queen said. "But as you wish. You may have your sapphire. It is on the table next to the door. I'm sure I do not have to tell you to take nothing else."

"Of course. Thank you, Your Majesty. You are generous and kind."

The cat inclined her head graciously. "I know. But it is good of you to say so. Now, I have one last question. Do you trust the wizard?"

Everyone seemed to ask the same question in the end. It worried her. "I... I do."

"Why?"

Before Angelina could answer, the cat faded into nothing, leaving her embroidery behind on the chair. The work was now complete. The last word read 'enough.'

Angelina got up and picked her way through the treasure room, stopping here and there to admire a piece that caught her eye. But no matter how lovely something was, she kept her hooves to herself and touched nothing.

As she approached the door, the shadows deepened until the light was nearly gone. Still, she could see the table where the sapphire lay. It was set into a ring and easy to pick up with her lips. She dropped it into her satchel and watched the door swing open.

The hall was utterly, deeply black. Angelina swallowed hard and shook her head, hoping the berries had a little more light left in them. But no, Valus had been right when he said they would only last an hour. Her conversation with Queen Felicity had taken far longer than that.

Angelina backed away from the door, fear clutching at her throat. Light flickered at the edge of her vision, and she turned her head. "What is that?" she whispered.

She turned and saw the loveliest, tiniest tiara she'd ever beheld. Silver filigree swirled with a miniature galaxy filled with stars and tiny planets. The whole thing glowed like a beacon in the dimly lit room.

If she wore that as she had the berry wreath, she'd be able to see her way out of the cave. It wouldn't be stealing if she left it inside the cave. Surely the queen would understand that she was only using it to light her way to the surface.

She turned to look back into the treasure room. "Hello? Queen Felicity? Valus? I... I need a light to show me the way out."

There was no answer. No one came to guide her or provide a new berry wreath. Angelina faced the door again. If she went into the hall with no light, she'd never find her way. She'd be lost in the caves forever.

She eyed the tiara. A book she'd read once stated that cats could see in the dark. Maybe Queen Felicity hadn't realized that unicorns couldn't.

Besides, stealing and borrowing were not the same thing. She'd leave it inside the cave. It would be fine.

Dipping her horn, she slipped it under the tiara and the little circlet glided down, settling perfectly onto her head. A halo of light fell around her, illuminating the ground at her feet.

The room shivered and groaned. *Thief.*

The whisper came from all around her, as if the treasure room itself was accusing her. The door creaked, the gap narrowing as she watched in horror.

Angelina bolted forward as the wood banged closed,

bruising her hindquarters as she slipped through.

"Thief!" The whisper became a shout, echoing off the rock walls as she ran. The tiara lit her way, showing her the tiny streams cascading down the walls turning into rivers.

She splashed through, her hooves sliding on the wet rock. If she didn't hurry, she'd be up to her knees in ice cold, churning black water. She ran on, ducking as the ceiling lowered and the walls narrowed, closing in on her, then suddenly widening. The path turned sharply, creating a deeper pond where the water swirled around her legs.

On her right was the sheer rock face. On her left, a plunging drop into the abyss. Shrieking, she pivoted, her hooves skidding close to the edge as water plummeted over, forming a waterfall, the current sucking at her hooves, trying to take her with it.

Terrified, she kept moving, hugging the wall even as the current tried to push her over.

All the while, the voice of the mountain shouted at her. "Thief! Robber! Return what you have stolen!"

"I'm not stealing it. Only borrowing," Angelina sobbed. Suddenly, she broke out of the corridor into the upper cave, its jagged teeth outlined starkly against the moonlit night beyond. She cried out in relief, but then gasped. The cave mouth was closing.

Rock ground against rock, the stones shrieking as if in pain, the red sand rippling under her feet as if it could taste her already.

Tossing her head, Angelina threw the tiara on the ground and sprinted for the closing entrance. "I'm sorry!" she cried and bolted between the teeth as they closed, catching the hair of her tail and tugging it painfully.

She collapsed onto the ground, crying pitifully. Nearby, a tapping crinkled the grass. She looked up to see Valus standing there, a disapproving frown on his mousy features. "I told you not to take anything other than what her grace gave you. What were you thinking?"

"That I needed light, so I wouldn't get lost."

He tossed a berry wreath at her. It landed on the ground and skidded to rest beneath her nose. "A light like this? I was bringing it to you, but you had taken the tiara, and were already gone."

Shame filled her and she could not meet his eyes. "I am sorry," she said.

"As you should be," he replied. Then, in a softer tone, he continued. "Learn who to trust, little unicorn. It is a hard lesson, but valuable."

A rustling of grass, and when she looked up, she was alone.

12: THE WIND

Angelina wandered through the woods, the berry wreath lighting her way, but her heart was heavy. Finally, too tired to go any further, she lay down beneath a giant oak tree and fell asleep.

Hours later, morning sunlight filtered through the leaves, along with the chatter of squirrels. Thousands of them.

They scampered along the branches, barreling around the trunk, catapulting between the leaves, arguing and challenging one another as they sprinted from bough to bough.

"You know you stole my acorns! Give them back or I will appeal to the High Climber himself!"

"I didn't! You just can't remember where you buried your stash!"

The pair scurried off, still arguing, as a quartet came into view.

"I tell you; cashews are better than walnuts any day."

"But really, Alfie, where are you going to get cashews in these woods?"

"Seb is right. They don't grow around here."

"But we could plant them, right?"

"Nope. Ya can't just plant any nuts you like and expect them to grow like that. Takes special magic for stuff like that…"

They passed into the upper reaches of the tree, leaving Angelina gaping in sleepy-eyed confusion.

"Thief!" One squirrel chased another under Angelina's nose and over her back, hollering all the way.

The other squirrel stopped dead, perched on Angelina's hip. "I am not a thief!" she said hotly. "You are the thief, stealing food from between my children's paws!"

The first squirrel's tail quivered in outrage. "I never ONCE stole from a youngling! But you—"

Angelina bolted to her feet, dumping both squirrels on the ground. They glared up at her before returning to their argument.

"We'll take this up with the High Climber!" they shouted together, and chased each other back up the tree, disappearing into the leaves while accusing one another of various crimes and misdemeanors.

"They're all crazy," Angelina muttered to herself.

She laid back down in the soft grass, trying to figure out what to do next. She still didn't know where Warbel was, and she didn't want to continue the journey without her. But Angelina missed her mom and sisters. She wanted to go home.

"What was next on the list?" she mused. "The wind. That's right. 'A bottle of wind in the midst of its blowing.' How do I get that?"

Just then, another squirrel, larger and considerably fatter than the others she'd seen, eased his way down the oak's mighty trunk. He wore a red velvet doublet and puffy pantaloons with gold stripes. A long crimson cloak attached to the doublet at the shoulders. It looked very fine indeed, but interfered with his climbing ability until he gruffly commanded three other squirrels to "Hold it up, won't you?" A gold crown sat askew between his ears, and he straightened it once he reached the ground.

"The High Climber, King of all Squirrels, comes!" the squirrels chanted. A great crowd gathered around the base of the tree, waiting for the king to descend.

Nine other squirrels in serious black robes jumped from limb to limb down the Oak behind him. Once they reached the ground, the entire scurry stalked toward her with all the squirrelish dignity they could muster.

Angelina worked hard not to giggle.

One of the black-robed squirrels stepped out from the rest and addressed her in a high-pitched voice. "Are you the Deliberate Earthquake?"

Angelina smiled at him. "I am a unicorn."

He sighed. "I can see that. Are you also a Deliberate Earthquake?"

Confused, Angelina's smile faded. "Well, I used to be a human girl, and I'd like to one be again, but I—"

"Yes, yes, all remarkably interesting, I'm sure. But what we want to know is, did you, or did you not, jump to your feet and dump Edith and Henry onto the ground on purpose a few moments ago?"

"Who are Edith and Henry?" Angelina's head hurt.

"Doesn't matter!" Another black-robed squirrel stepped forward. "She's obviously not an earthquake, deliberate or otherwise. Earthquakes don't have horns."

Angelina blinked at him. "Of course I'm not an earthquake."

The squirrel beamed at her. "See? Told you."

A robeless squirrel leaped out of the crowd. "But you dumped us on the ground. Rude, it was!"

Angelina recognized him as the squirrel who had perched on her hip. She pawed the ground. "You scampered over my chest and sat on my hip without even asking. Talk about rude!"

The High Climber glared at the robeless one. "Is that true?"

"Well, yes, but she was just lying there. We didn't think she'd mind."

"That's ridiculous," Angelina said. "You'd mind if I sat on your hip, right?"

"Of course I would. But you are several hundred times my size, so you'd likely crush me. Big difference," he pointed out reasonably.

"No, no, no," the High Climber said. "Consent always matters. You did not get consent; therefore, your suit is moot. Court dismissed. I'm late for my massage. You three." He pointed at three random squirrels without robes. "Help me with my cloak."

The squirrels all dispersed, the black-robed ones going much slower than the rest, since their clothes kept them from scampering well.

"Wait," Angelina said. "I have a question."

The High Climber turned to frown at her. "Well? Hurry now. Haven't all day, you know." The black-robed squirrels came back.

"Do you know where I can find the wind to trap it in a bottle?"

He raised a bushy eyebrow. "All of it? I only ask because the wind has important work to do, and if you take all of it, that could prove problematic for the rest of us."

"Oh, I see. Well, no. I don't need it all, just a little. Even a breeze would probably do," Angelina replied.

"I see. It is an interesting question," the High Climber said. "I shall inquire of my council." He turned to the black-robed squirrels. "What say you?"

"Well, first, she'll need better clothes," the first said. "The wind is very particular about his companions. He won't come to just anyone."

"What?" Angelina said. "That's ridic—"

"Hush, unicorn. We are advising the king," said a second squirrel. "I believe it is more important that she get a manicure. Can you imagine the wind allowing himself to be captured by such unprepossessing hooves?"

Angelina stared at her hooves in dismay. It was true. The journey had not been kind to them.

The other squirrels chuckled and a third spoke up. "No, no, it's all quite impossible. Unicorns are meant to be ridden by fair maidens. To suggest any other task for them is ludicrous."

"I'm not being ridden by anyone, fair maidens included," Angelina grumped.

"What about a handsome lad? I hear they are quite nice and make interesting companions," another squirrel asked.

"Ugh," Angelina said.

"No, no, it has to be a fair maiden," the first squirrel insisted. "All the stories say so."

The High Climber sighed as the council fell to arguing the merits of handsome lads over fair maidens. Angelina realized she'd never get the answers she needed from any of them and took the opportunity to walk away.

Looking up into the sky, she noticed the sun was setting. She must have spent longer with the squirrels, and wandered further from them, than she thought. Indeed, the massive oak was gone from sight and the chittering of the squirrels lost in the distance.

Now the forest whispered to her. Oaks and maples, birches and pines swayed together in the rising wind. The sky painted her cloud garments scarlet and gold as the sun began its descent.

The wind picked up as evening came on, sifting through the tree leaves. Then she saw Warbel above her, riding the breeze higher and higher. She barely had to flap her wings; it was so strong.

A zephyr swept down, ruffling Angelina's mane and tickling her chin whiskers playfully. It caught some flower petals and wove them into the strands. Angelina laughed.

Why hadn't she seen it before? She didn't have to go anywhere. The wind was all around her. All she had to do was figure out a way to bottle some of it.

Opening her pack, she nuzzled about inside and came up with a little glass cylinder, its top stoppered with a cork plug. Pinning the bottle between her hooves, she carefully pried the cork free with her teeth. When she stepped away, the bottle fell over.

Gently, carefully, she picked it up with her lips, maneuvering the glass so that the open end pointed out. As she bent to lift the bottle from the ground, a petal fell into it from her beard.

The wind whistled into the bottle, making the petal dance and jump inside the glass. Now, how was she going to put the cap on?

Warbel swooped down, plucking up the cork in her beak. She shoved it into the neck of the bottle. "Brilliant," she trilled. "I knew you'd figure it out."

"I wish I'd known," Angelina grumbled.

"Ah, dear unicorn girl. All you had to do was trust yourself, as I've done all along."

"That's nice to hear. I was worried, when you flew off, that you might not come back." Angelina flopped down on a patch of grass and flowers. She was hungry and thirsty, but at least they had the first three items on the list.

"Not come back? Why would I do that? We have a pact, you and me. I'll see it through to the end."

"Good to know. I could have used some of that dedication with the sapphire."

The wren hopped about on a branch. "I told you; I couldn't go with you on that part. You got the stone, yes?"

"No thanks to you. That cave almost ate me, you know."

"Oh, the cave wouldn't have eaten you."

"You don't know that. Did you see its teeth?" Angelina felt a cold shudder run through her just thinking about it.

"I have seen the teeth, but it's all for show. The cave is

a vegetarian."

"It's… what?"

"A vegetarian. Only eats plants and the occasional bug. But that's on accident, or so it claims. Besides, Valus was there. He wouldn't let you get hurt."

Angelina rolled her eyes. "You could have told me that before you took off. I needed your help. And things aren't getting any easier." Angelina chewed her lower lip.

The first ingredient had been a challenge. The second ended up being downright dangerous, but that was her own fault. Getting the wind in a bottle had turned out to be simple enough, but there were still two ingredients to go.

Catching a sun ray was going to be the hardest task yet, she just knew it.

"What do you mean?" Warbel asked. "You've only got two more things to find."

"Yes, but a ray of sun? The tears of a banshee? How am I going to get those?"

"Same way you got the first two. Go to the person who has them and ask politely."

Angelina pawed the ground nervously. "And I suppose you know exactly who controls the sun?"

"Oh, we don't need to go all the way to Helios' palace," Warbel said. "The throne room of the Queen of Dawn will be far enough."

"Another queen?" Angelina was glad she was laying down. Her legs felt funny, like they wouldn't support her if she tried to stand.

Warbel laughed. "Don't worry. You'll like Aurora. She's nice."

Angelina settled her head on her forelegs and closed her eyes. "That's what I thought about Felicity, until her house tried to eat me," she muttered just before she fell asleep.

13: THE SUN'S RAYS

"Wake up, Angelina. We have a long journey ahead of us."
The sharp rap of Warbel's beak against her horn startled the
unicorn awake, and she sat up abruptly.

Warbel tumbled into the air with a cry. "Easy there,
friend! You nearly skewered me with that thing!"

"Your own fault," Angelina replied grumpily. "Didn't
anyone ever tell you it's dangerous to wake a sleeping
unicorn?"

Warbel trilled a laugh. "They have, and now I know
it's true. Come on. There's a berry patch over there, and
some carrots growing next to it. Eat quickly and we'll be on
our way."

Angelina wobbled to her feet and ran a tongue over her
teeth. She never thought she'd miss her toothbrush, but her
teeth felt mossy, and she wished she could clean them.
Still, carrots ought to help. She ambled toward the berries
Warbel mentioned. Between the fruit and the carrots, she
was soon full.

It wasn't long before she and the wren were back on
the forest path, heading east toward the rising sun.

"Why did we have to leave so early?" Angelina asked

after a while.

"Because we must reach the shore before dark so we can be there at sunrise tomorrow morning. It's the only way to reach the Dawn Queen's court."

Angelina frowned. "The Queen of Dawn holds court on the forest's eastern shore?"

The bird wobbled, her wings losing their steady beat for an instant. She steadied herself and cast Angelina a sidelong glance. "Not exactly," she said.

No matter how Angelina poked and prodded, Warbel would say nothing more on the subject and, after a few more attempts, the unicorn girl let it drop.

As they traveled, the oaks and maples gave way to sago palms and kudzu vines. The soil grew sandy underfoot, with the occasional crunch of seashells and sea glass growing more and more frequent. Finally, as the sun set once more, they reached the shore.

Angelina looked around. There was no house, just a long, wide stretch of white sand and curling waves. The ocean stretched all the way to the horizon, with the moon casting wavering silver streaks across the water. The sun's last rays disappeared behind them, leaving the pair in starlight and moonbeams for the night.

"Now what?" she asked Warbel as the bird settled on a nearby palm branch.

"Now we get some rest. We must rise before dawn if we are to have enough rays to cross the full distance."

Angelina stared at her friend, but the wren curled into the palm leaves and tucked her head under her wing, pretending to be asleep and refusing to explain.

After trotting all day, Angelina was exhausted, so she settled into the soft sand and used a pile of dried seaweed for a pillow. It smelled of sun and brine, but it was soft enough. Between one breath and the next, Angelina fell asleep.

The moon was still peeking through the palms when Warbel tapped on her horn to wake her. Angelina sat up grumpily. Being wakened before dawn two days in a row was doing nothing for her disposition. When this was over, she was going to sleep for a week.

"Warbel, the sun isn't even up yet. Why do I have to wake up now?"

"Because you must be awake and ready when the first ray stretches across the water."

"Why?"

"Because her castle lies due east from here," Warbel said patiently. "Across the water."

"But…" Angelina looked around. "How am I going to get there? There's no boat."

"You will not need a boat."

"Then how am going to get across?" She huffed a laugh. "It's not like I can walk on water."

Warbel didn't laugh. "You won't need to walk on water. You'll be running on sunbeams."

Angelina stared at him. "I'll be running on what?"

A suggestion of light glimmered on the horizon and Warbel hopped on the branch. "Listen carefully. When the first ray of sunlight reaches the shore, you must race along it toward the sun as fast as you can go. It will not be wide, so you must keep a straight course. Do not veer right or left so much a hoof beat, or you will fall into the ocean and drown."

Angelina stared at her in disbelief. "I can't run on sunbeams. They aren't solid!"

"Who says?"

Angelina paused. She couldn't remember where or when she'd first heard that sunbeams weren't solid. She just knew they weren't. But even if they were…

"Well, OK, let's say you're right. They don't last long enough for a human to run on them."

"You are correct for a couple of reasons. One, the beams themselves don't last long. Once they reach the shore, they dispense their light and are no longer thick enough to travel on. And two, once the sun rises to a certain point, the rays fragment when they hit the water, scattering into sparkles instead of beams of light. No one can run on sparkles except water fae. Even they don't try it often. So, you'll only have a short amount of time to make the journey."

"See, I told you. Impossible."

Warbel winked at her. "Impossible for a horse or a goat, perhaps. But you are neither of those things. You are a unicorn. And unicorns are the fastest hooved creatures in the universe. And you can get quite far on a single ray of light." She glanced nervously at the horizon. "But even so, you are right. One ray won't be enough."

"So, what happens when one runs out?"

The bird chirped at her. "You leap to the next, of course."

Angelina looked to the horizon, where the sun's first tentative rays were stretching across the dark water. None had reached the near shore yet, but the first was only seconds away. "Sunlight is hot. It will burn me."

"Nonsense. It doesn't burn you to walk under the sun on a cloudless day, does it?" Warbel said.

"No, because Mom always makes me wear sunscreen."

"Fine, but even if she doesn't, it takes a while, right? It gets hotter as you approach the court, but you'll be fine as long as you keep moving. At least, I think you will… for the most part."

For the most part? What about the other parts? "I can't do this," she said.

Warbel let out a breath and her feathers slumped. "Then you will not get the rays you need. Helios would never give them to you, but Aurora might, if you are brave and true."

Angelina approached the water's edge and stared at the glow on the horizon. "It will blind me before I'm halfway there."

"You need not look at the sun itself, only on the next step before you. You can do this, Angelina. I believe in you."

Just then, the first golden ray leaped from the horizon and sprinted across the water, making a straight path to the nearer shore.

"Are you ready?" Warbel trilled. "You must race to meet it, leap upon it as soon as it is close enough, then run as fast as you can. When it flickers, jump to the next ray and run faster. Jump and run, run and jump until you reach the farther shore.

"I can't even see the farther shore." Muscles tensing, Angelina watched the sunbeam race toward her. This was crazy. A person couldn't run on a sunbeam.

Could they?

The ray was twenty feet from shore when she started running. A featherlight touch settled next to her horn, and she realized Warbel was going with her. She reached the water's edge and leaped, sailing through the air to land with a... clatter of hooves.

She slowed, the shock of landing on a sunbeam and finding it solid jolting through her, even as her hooves kept moving.

"Don't stop!" Warbel shouted. "RUN!"

Angelina ran. Sparks flew up where her hooves touched, but the sunbeam was surprisingly strong and wide. She kept her gaze down, training it on the path ahead as she sprinted along.

"Keep to the center," Warbel shouted.

Angelina could see why. As she ran, the beam narrowed. When she glanced up, she could see it ended in the distance. A quick glance over her shoulder told her it was fading behind her. She couldn't go back, and she was running out of room ahead.

Already the water around her was deep, though clear. It was probably over her head. She could still swim to shore from here. Maybe she should turn around.

"Don't slow down!" Warbel shouted. "When you reach the end, jump to the next ray!"

Angelina looked and, sure enough, another ray was racing toward the first, their ends sure to connect if the first didn't fade to nothing first. She just had to get there before that happened.

She ran faster, the wind whipping her tail and beard like a hurricane.

The beam flickered, and her front hoof splashed in salt water. She jumped, soaring through the air to land with a splash and a clatter. She'd made it, but she couldn't stop to be glad.

She ran on.

Run, splash, jump, splash, run… It wasn't long before Angelina's sides were heaving, her hooves heavy as lead. She didn't dare look for the distant shore, but she was certain it was too far. She'd never make it.

"Faster, Angelina. The sun rises and you are too big to run on sparkles."

She wanted to tell the wren that she was already going as fast as she could, but she didn't have the breath to waste. She ran faster.

The rays were thinner now, with tiny gaps in them. Sparkles drifted from them, lovely and bright and terrifying.

The water was dark around her, black-deep and cold.

She tried to ignore the even darker shapes swimming under the sunbeams. If she fell in now, she'd never make it back to shore. She was too far out.

She stumbled, sending fragments of glittering sunlight spinning off into the depths. Catching herself, she ran on.

"Careful," Warbel said. "You got the berries. You found the gem. You figured out the wind all on your own. You can do this."

"It's. Too. Far," she gasped. "I'll never. Make it."

"You are closer than you think. Don't give up. Keep going."

Was the water a little clearer now? A little more blue than black? No, she was imagining it. She was so tired. She just wanted it to be done.

Splash. The sunbeam flickered.

"Jump, Angelina!" Warble yelled.

But there was nothing to jump to. The next ray flickered too, and then scattered into glittering sparkles, dusting the ocean's surface like stars, and Angelina fell.

"Swim," Warbel cried. "You are almost there. You can make it."

Angelina kicked feebly, trying to swim, forcing her legs to move, to keep her afloat. Her hoof struck something, pushing it aside, and a cloud of golden brown swirled around her legs as a second hoof found purchase.

She dragged herself forward, one step, two. The water was throat high, then chest high. It eddied around her knees, the sand sucking from under her feet as it washed back out to the ocean. She stumbled to the shore and collapsed.

14: QUEEN OF THE DAWN

Angelina couldn't open her eyes. Weariness weighed them down.

"Bring her to the hall. We can make her comfortable there until her room is ready." The voice was kind and gentle, but with a strength that made Angelina feel safe and cared for. Nothing could hurt her so long as the owner of such a voice was near.

Time passed. Angelina couldn't tell how long, but the place was warm, and smelled of bread baking and fresh pasta sauce cooking. "Mom?" Angelina murmured.

"Wake up!" Warbel whispered loudly from close by. "It wasn't that bad, and you are embarrassing me. You are a unicorn, for pity's sake!"

"Leave her alone, Warbel. A person capable of such heroic effort deserves whatever rest she needs."

"Heroic effort? She collapsed on your front steps!"

"She raced the dawn and won. That is commendable. She did so on faith alone — faith in you, I might add — so you need not be so harsh with her."

When Warbel spoke again, she sounded less impatient. "She did, didn't she? I'm sorry for my tone, Your Grace. In truth, I am worried about her. If only she'd wake, I could see that she is all right, and that would bring me comfort."

"I know," the other voice said. "But pushing someone to act against their own wellbeing is not kind, my friend."

"As you say, Your Grace," Warbel replied, so subdued and remorseful that Angelina felt sorry for her.

The unicorn forced her eyes open and sat up. Beneath her was a wool blanket, soft and warm, in hues of blue and green. Under that stretched a pink and white marble floor.

"Ah, my dear, you are awake."

Angelina followed the voice to a woman so beautiful she had to blink twice to be sure she wasn't hallucinating. Red-gold curls fell around pale shoulders. The woman's wide, blue eyes stared at Angelina with curiosity and compassion. High cheekbones and full, red lips made her the picture of a storybook queen. But her clothes…

She wore a white lab coat over dark green slacks, and a pair of safety goggles perched on top of her head. Sensible sneakers enclosed her feet and a pair of gloves hung from the pocket of her lab coat.

Jewels glinted in her other pocket and Angelina blinked again. *What is that?* She wondered.

She didn't get the chance to ask.

"Welcome to my laboratory," the woman said. "I am Aurora, Queen of the Dawn." She gestured to the room, and Angelina followed the movement to look around the room. Tables set up around the space held experiments in various stages of completion. Funnels and bottles, some connected with rubber tubing, sat in deliberate groups. Conical flasks on Bunsen burners sat next to microscopes with stacks of slides waiting for examination. A lab tech at each table entered data into a computer.

Angelina stared in wonder. "This is a science lab," she said in wonder.

"Of course," Aurora said. "The dawn pretty much handles itself. I had to have something to do with my brain." She slipped off the lab coat and hung it up on a coat rack. In the same movement, she took a long, multi-colored cape and slung it around her shoulders.

Angelina gasped. Elaborately embroidered mathematical symbols done in all the colors of the dawn, from palest pink to indigo, covered the cloak. Between the symbols were suns, the tiny rays glimmering gold against the cream fabric.

Reaching into the pocket of her lab coat, Aurora pulled out a silver crown and exchanged it for the safety goggles. With a wave of her hand, all the tables retreated gracefully to the walls.

An ivory throne slid forward from some hidden place, gliding to a halt behind the queen.

Aurora mounted three steps, swept the cloak to one side, and sat down. She took a scepter from its holder on the throne and smoothed the green silk dress she'd been wearing under her lab coat.

Angelina blinked again. *Wasn't she wearing pants a minute ago?*

Warbel fluttered in and perched on the back of the queen's throne.

Queen Aurora was a vision. She was everything one can imagine a queen to be. Beautiful, graceful, wise and kind. Looking at her on that ivory throne, Angelina suddenly felt rumpled, dirty and ugly. What was she doing here, asking for favors from someone like this?

She hung her head and close her eyes, wishing fervently that the floor would open and swallow her whole.

Footsteps echoed across the marble floor and green skirts appeared within Angelina's field of vision. Soft fingers touched her chin and lifted her face.

"This is my mirror. Look into it."

The last thing Angelina wanted right then was a mirror, but this was Queen Aurora. She looked. And then she blinked and looked again.

"What do you see?" Queen Aurora asked.

"I see… me."

"And what do you look like? Come now. You have no option but to be honest. That is the magic of the mirror. It is honest and brings that quality out of the viewer as well."

"I look like… a beautiful human girl," Angelina said softly. "I am a few months past ten with blue eyes and short, dark hair. I have nice skin and a strong frame."

"Yes," the queen replied. "But the mirror shows more. Look deeper."

Angelina blushed and ducked her head.

The queen smiled. "Shall I tell you what I see? I see honest eyes and a heart that is true, even when it might serve you better to be sly, and inconstant." She tucked the mirror away and sat next to Angelina on her blanket. "You are lovely in your own right. Do not let anyone make you doubt it."

Angelina nodded.

Aurora clapped her hands and a host of servants rolled in tables heaped with food. As they ate, Aurora asked about Angelina's journey.

"Well, it all started the morning I woke up a unicorn," Angelina said. She told the rest of her adventures, ending with, "But I don't see how one can capture a ray of sun. Even running on a sunbeam was difficult. They just don't last that long." She glanced up, hoping she hadn't offended. "Begging your pardon, Your Grace."

"Never apologize for speaking the truth. They are fragile things, sunbeams, unless fixed in place with magic. Fortunately for you, I have just the thing." Aurora plucked a golden thread from her robe, drawing it out carefully so it didn't break. With equal care, she leaned over and wove it into Angelina's mane. With a gesture and a word, the act was complete.

"Now, it won't come out until you want it to."

"Thank you, Your Majesty."

"No trouble at all. Now, you'll sleep here tonight, and my roc will give you a ride back to the mainland in the morning."

Angelina all but fell off her hooves with relief, knowing she wouldn't have to race the dawn again.

Servants came and led her upstairs to a comfortable bed, where she slept soundly and without dreams that she remembered. The next day, Queen Aurora and Warbel met her on the shore. A giant black bird stood quietly nearby.

Servants wheeled a giant staircase up and Angelina climbed it carefully. The roc's saddle had been built with unicorns in mind. It was shaped like a large square bowl, with safety straps and a small safety compartment for Warbel.

As they strapped Angelina in, Aurora spoke. "I have one more question for you."

"Ma'am?"

"This wizard. Do you trust him?"

Angelina hesitated. "I… um… Yes?"

"Why?"

The pilot slapped the reins, and the roc leaped into the air; his great black wings flung wide. Angelina looked down, but the queen was already gone.

"Everyone asks, but no one waits for an answer," Angelina said. "Why do you think that is, Warbel?"

"Why, indeed?" Warbel said, as if she had no answers.

15: THE BANSHEE'S TEARS

As the roc landed, Angelina checked her satchel again. The berries, sapphire and bottle of wind were all tucked into pockets inside.

The pilot released her straps and opened the door of Warbel's compartment. Angelina's feet had barely touched the sand when the roc leaped into the air. Bits of shell and seaweed flew around her ankles and Angelina squinted against the sandy wind his wings stirred up.

Warbel clung to her horn until the wind died down. Then she helped Angelina remove the ray of sun Aurora had given her from her mane and tuck it into a second bottle, which they secured next to the first. All was safe and secure.

Only one ingredient remained.

The tears of the banshee.

Slowly, Angelina turned away from the ocean and began the search for the last ingredient. For a while she concentrated on avoiding the palm fronds that overhung the path, but eventually, the sand became soil, and the palms gave way to oaks and maples again.

"Do you know where to find the banshee?" she asked

Warbel.

"I have never been there, but they say her hovel sits in the midst of the deepest bog in the forest. A wide marsh surrounds it – a treacherous place with many dangers – easy to get lost in. There are two ways to get to her hut."

Angelina tried to look at him, but only ended up crossing her eyes. She looked down at the path. "And those are?"

"The first way is through the swamp. You hop from hummock to hummock, but those move when you least expect it, trying to dump you into the brackish water."

"Sounds delightful," Angelina replied sourly.

"Not as delightful as the kelpies that live in that water. I've heard they mostly eat fish, but will take any meat they can get."

"Perfect. I can't hop on the hummocks, and I can't swim between them. How am I supposed to get to her house?" She was walking through the forest now, sunlight dappling the path through the tall trees. She stopped in a clearing to search for vegetables or berries, finding enough to stop the hunger pangs her stomach was sending to her.

"There is the second way, The Path of Temptation," Warbel said. "But it is narrow and has dangers of its own."

"Of course it does. Why can't anything be easy?"

"Breathing is easy, and you do that without thinking. Would you want to approach a banshee without thinking?" Warbel asked.

"No, I guess not."

"Things worth doing are often challenging. That doesn't mean they aren't important. This is the last task, Angelina. And remember, you aren't alone."

"I know," she said. "Thank you. I think I'll take the path. At least I can be sure of keeping my feet under me that way."

By mid-afternoon, the ground under her feet was soft and spongy. Moss hung from the trees in long, tangled skeins like hair that hadn't seen a comb in months. The trees closed in, shutting out the sunlight until she wished she had her crown of light berries back.

When her hooves sank into the muck, Angelina drew back with a tiny squeal.

"We have to turn here," Warbel said. "Travel the edge of the bog until we find the path. But there is something else we have to do first. Wait here."

The wren flew off, leaving Angelina gaping after her. Cold, bitter rain fell, making Angelina shiver. She shrank closer to the tree, hoping the thick leaves would shelter her while she waited.

A song floated to her on the wind, melodic and enchanting. The singers sounded so happy. She looked toward the sound, but at first, she could see no one. As she listened, the words grew louder.

> *Come now, come now, join the dance*
> *See our hoof beats, see us prance,*
> *Golden white, happy, and bright,*
> *Come and join us now tonight.*

The voices were light and filled with laughter. Peering through the trees, Angelina could make out the shadows of people dancing around a fire, their hands joined as they circled. They looked so warm. She took a step toward them.

> *Come to dance and join the feast*
> *We are here for your sweet taste,*
> *See your worth to our delight,*
> *Come and join us, now tonight.*

Angelina's mouth watered. She was hungry. She wanted to dance! It looked like such fun. She didn't notice that her hooves were slipping into the muck, didn't smell the swamp clinging to her fetlocks, didn't feel the cold sinking into her bones.

Icy water splashed in her eyes and a flutter of wings broke against her face. "Angelina!" Warbel shouted. "Stop! Don't listen to them!"

The song turned to hissing, and the human shapes shifted into black horses. But not the sleek, glossy beauties she'd seen in the fields at home. These were gaunt creatures out of a nightmare, with long, sharp teeth and cloven hooves. Bog slime matted their coats and tangles of water weeds knotted their manes. Each one wore a silver halter, and they hissed at her when she backed away.

"Those are kelpies," she whispered.

"Yes." Warbel flew backward in front of her, keeping the kelpies from making eye-contact, making sure that Angelina kept moving away from them, back toward drier ground.

"They were going to eat me."

"Yes."

The earth was damp, but firm under Angelina's hooves now. The rain had stopped. Warbel got her turned around and moving in the right direction. The kelpie's song drifted to her, tugging at her.

"Hold still," Warbel said. "I'm going to put this in your ears."

He fluttered around her head, and she shied away, flicking her ears. "What is it?"

"Beeswax. Hold still." He fluttered close, and she felt something warm and soft being poked into her ear. It felt weird, and she had to fight the urge to shake her head.

"Why?" Her voice sounded odd. Half muffled and echoey. Warbel moved to the other side of her head to repeat the process.

Seconds later, it was as if she'd plunged her head underwater. She could hear, but the sound was muted. She could understand words, but the wax robbed them of inflection.

"There," Warbel said. "That should keep you safe. At

least from the kelpies."

"Thank you, Warbel." Angelina said. She shivered, thinking of what would have happened if the wren had not returned in time.

"What?" Warbel asked. "I've put wax in my ears too, so I can't hear very well."

"What?" Angelina said. "You've put wax in my ears, remember? Can't hear very well."

They stared at each other and then burst out laughing.

"Well," Warbel said after a moment. "As long as we can laugh, I think we'll be all right."

"What?" Angelina said.

16: THE BANSHEE

They found the path to the banshee's hovel just as the sun was setting. Instead of trying for it at night, they sparked a fire and made a little hut out of tree branches to rest for the night.

After some loud and confusing discussion, they took the wax out of one ear each. That way they could talk to each other and listen for other dangers but had the option of replacing the wax quickly if any kelpies showed up.

The next morning they were both awake early. Neither had slept well. Between the damp ground and the fear of being eaten by water demons, it hadn't been a restful night.

Before he put the wax back in her ears, Warbel gave Angelina a final warning. "Keep to the path. It goes straight to her hovel, but there are inviting branches and—" She hesitated. "Other things to tempt you. Don't follow them, no matter what you see or how much better the new path looks."

"I understand," Angelina said.

Warbel hovered in front of her. "Angelina, please, remember what happened when you ignored Valus' advice?"

The memory of cave teeth crashing down, ripping out some of her tail hairs, skittered through her mind and Angelina closed her eyes. "I remember. I won't make that mistake again, I promise."

"Good. Now, one last thing. Like all fae, the banshee loves making deals, and she'll try to make one with you. Don't do it."

"But what if it's a good deal?"

"It will sound like an excellent deal. She'll promise you what you want most in all the world, but the cost…" The wren perched on a nearby branch, her chest rising in deep sigh. "She will make it sound entirely reasonable and fair. But it won't be, trust me. The cost is always too high."

"Don't wander from the path, don't make any deals. Got it." Angelina nodded once, twice, her horn bobbing.

Warbel trilled. "Good. And if you get into trouble, shout. I'll be with you, just out of sight. Remember, no matter how it seems, you are not alone."

Angelina stood at the head of the trail. It extended, narrow but straight, into the heart of the bog.

Pools of scum-crusted water ponded on either side. Hummocks of sedge and creeping wildrye grass rose from the water, all looking solid enough to stand on. And maybe some of them were. But the swamp loved to deceive and Warbel had told her that until you put your foot on it, you couldn't tell which ground was solid, and which was simply an illusion, meant to suck you under.

As she scanned the swamp, Angelina caught movement out of the corner of her eye. She watched a heron try to step from a little island to a nearby hummock. The clump of sedge and dirt lurched sideways at the last minute, dumping the heron into the murky water. The bird thrashed once, twice, and went under. A few bubbles and several feathers rose to the surface, but the heron didn't.

Angelina shuddered and decided the path was just fine, narrow or not.

Black cypress and Ash trees hunched over the trail, casting it in deep shadows. As far as she could see, nothing moved. Silence descended on the bog that she didn't think had anything to do with the wax in her ears.

Angelina swallowed hard and set her foot on the path. As she walked, she did her best to keep her eyes on the trail ahead. If she didn't look right or left, she reasoned, she couldn't be tempted.

Something splashed to her right, and automatically, she turned her head. A pebble-strewn walkway led from the path to a charming little house. Outside, rocking in a miniature rocker, was a bright winged fae. The tiny creature jumped up, smiling and beckoning.

She couldn't be the banshee, could she? All the tales said banshees were horrid creatures, wicked and ugly in their black hooded robes.

Angelina hesitated. The nixie rose up, flashing wicked sharp teeth and a bright, slashing sword in her hand. Startled, Angelina drew back, surprised to find that she had stopped with her front feet on the walkway, her rear ones still on the trail.

Quickly, the girl-turned-unicorn returned to the path and moved off. The wax in her ears deadened the shrill screeching of the nixie's laughter, but she could still hear it.

"Mean thing," Angelina muttered.

Now she hurried as the sun rose toward its apex. Warbel had said she should reach the banshee's cabin by noon, so she should be almost there. The trail never curved or turned, but cut straight as an arrow flies through the bog.

Angelina saw a few more nixies, and more than one kelpie tried to lure her from the path, but she only trotted faster, ignoring them.

There were turnoffs, each one prettier than the last. One had sweetly scented yellow flowers along both sides. Another had what looked like her favorite cookies growing on long green stems.

That had been tempting, since she was getting hungry, but she bit her lip and ignored it.

"Anything that looks good in this place is probably poisonous anyway," she said to herself, and trotted on.

Then she came to a fork in the road. The path ahead was straight, but to her right...

A flash of wild hair and a long, pink skirt.

"Mom?" Angelina stopped dead in the road. She stared at the woman standing on the detour. She was carrying a basket of food on one arm and a blanket on the other. The food smelled delicious. "Mama?" Angelina's voice came out barely a squeak. She missed her mom so much.

The woman beckoned. "Yes, it's me. Come. I brought you some good things to eat."

Angelina took a step toward her. She looked behind the woman, and to both sides. Something was missing. She stopped. "Where are my sisters? Where are Marianna and HollyAnne?"

Frowning, the woman put the basket down next to the path and started spreading out the blanket. "I wanted us to have some alone time, so they stayed home," she said. "Don't worry. They'll be fine on their own for a bit."

Angelina backed up. This wasn't right. Mama would never leave Mari and Holly alone for more than a few minutes. She rarely left Angelina alone long enough to run to Wally's Grocery, and that was just on the corner, not more than a minute or two from their front door.

"No," she said. "I don't know what or who you are. But you aren't my mom."

"Angelina Smith!" The woman bounced to her feet; her features set in stern lines. "You come here right now. I've come all this way, gone to all this trouble. The least you can do is try some of this wonderful food I've brought you."

Angelina stopped. She looked over her shoulder. "What is my middle name?"

The woman's face darkened with anger. "Don't be disrespectful. Come here, immediately."

Angelina started walking. "You aren't my mother. She would have answered me." She tossed another glance over her shoulder, this one at the basket, and shuddered. "And she wouldn't have made me eat that!" The contents of the basket writhed, black and red and hissing.

Picking up the pace, Angelina galloped up the trail. She heard nothing more behind her and when she looked back, the woman, the basket and the blanket were all gone.

A little further on, she saw it.

A huge hummock, and perched on top, the rattiest, most tumbledown hovel ever built. The thatch roof sagged, and the chimney listed to the side, with several bricks missing. The front door hung askew, and the windows were crooked. The front steps were missing two of their treads. Caulking fell away from between the stones, leaving gaps for the wind to thrust its cold hands through. Whatever else she might know, Angelina knew she wouldn't want to sleep a night under that roof.

In the clearing out front stood an old woman dressed in a tattered black gown, belted at the waist with a bit of rope. Her gray-black hair straggled unbound over her shoulders, and a peaked black hat with a wide brim hid her features.

She stirred something in a huge, black cauldron over an open fire, and as she stirred, she sang.

> *Children's bones and a little dog's fur,*
> *Broken promises, and essence of myrrh,*
> *Little girl's tears and a big man's fears,*
> *That's been my dinner, for many a year.*

As the unicorn stepped into the clearing, the singing stopped. Angelina shivered.

She'd found the banshee.

The woman turned slowly; the huge paddle she'd been

using to stir the pot clenched in her gnarled hands. Angelina fought back a gasp.

The woman was horribly ugly. She had a long, hooked nose that nearly touched her chin. On it were two warts, one with a long, stringy hair sprouting from the center. Her eyes were squinty, her chin pointed and sharp. And one tooth hung over her thin lower lip as if trying to nail her mouth shut. It wasn't successful.

"Who are you and what do you want? And don't lie to me, girl. I'll know if you lie, and I don't have time for foolishness."

"Why do you call me a girl? Everyone else thinks I'm a unicorn," Angelina said. "At least, they do at first."

"Then they're idiots," the hag snapped. "Anyone can see that someone's cursed you into a body that isn't your own."

Angelina stiffened. Not only was this person ugly, she was rude. "My friends are not idiots."

"Your friends, are they? Then why didn't they turn you back?"

"Most of them don't know how. Why don't you?" Angelina asked.

"I'm not your friend," the hag said. "And I don't do favors for free." Her black eyes glittered, and her voice grew oily with greed. "But if you can pay, perhaps we can make a deal."

A trill from overhead made Angelina's ears prick up, but she was already shaking her head. "I'm not here to make a deal," she said.

"Then what do you want?" the banshee grumped. "I'm a busy fae and I don't have time to play games with foolish girls."

"If I am to become human again, I must gather five ingredients for the spell that will return me to myself," Angelina said. "I've gotten the first four, but now I need the last one."

"And what is that?" the banshee asked.

"I need some of your tears," Angelina replied, and the creature threw back her head and roared with laughter.

"Why are you laughing?" Angelina asked. "None of this is funny."

The banshee held her belly and gave a great sigh. "I haven't cried in a thousand years, so I doubt I'll cry for you. You're welcome to try, though. Go ahead. Try." The evil creature leered at Angelina. "But if you fail, into the pot you go. I love a good unicorn stew, you know."

Instead of nodding or replying in any way that the banshee could interpret as agreement, Angelina backed a few steps away and tried to think of a way to make the banshee cry.

First, she tried to think of things that made most people cry. "Stubbing my toe or falling in the skinning my knees makes me cry," she murmured.

"Eh? What's that?" the banshee asked irritably.

"Nothing, nothing, just thinking out loud."

"Well, stop it. Dead irritating, it is."

As awful as she was, Angelina didn't want to hurt the banshee, so skinned knees and stubbed toes were out, especially since she couldn't think of a way to make either of them happen. Shoving her over would probably just make her angry, anyway.

When was the last time I cried when I wasn't hurt? She asked herself. And an idea came to her.

"I have a story to tell you," she said to the banshee.

"It better be a good one." the creature went back to stirring the pot with her giant spoon.

Angelina told the banshee the saddest stories she could think of, but nothing moved her. Not the Tale of the Mother, or The Babes in the Wood. Even the Children of Llyr didn't bring a single tear to the banshee's eye, though Angelina almost shed a few while telling it.

Story after story Angelina told, each one sadder than

the last, but the banshee laughed through each one. "I will have a lovely meal tonight," she cackled as Angelina finished the tale of the Little Mermaid, (the original, in which the mermaid dies, not the modern version.)

There are no stories left, Angelina thought. *I'll never see my sisters or my mother again. Agreement or no, the banshee won't let me leave here. I'm going to die in these woods and this horrible creature will throw me in a pot and eat me.*

Her eyes filled with tears, and they trickled down her cheeks. The banshee looked up, startled. "Here now. I thought I was the one supposed to cry. What ails you, girl?" she asked.

So, Angelina told her.

She started at the beginning, waking up with a pillow stuck to her horn and not being able to properly brush her teeth. She spoke of the mean Mrs. Finchhagle and being chased by the Air Force into the woods.

She described the wizard's hut and the eagle's aerie. Her tale wound through scraped knees and the loss of her tail hairs in the cave's terrible teeth. She related her terror on the ocean, jumping from sunbeam to sunbeam and the awful danger swimming below her.

She spoke of the wren's loyalty and wise advice, her own mistakes, and the lessons she learned along the way. Last of all, she cried when she talked about her family and how she missed them. Her tears came fast and hard when she spoke of her fear that she would never see her mother again.

Through it all, the banshee sat entranced. All the other stories had been distant, created from time and fantasy. Perhaps they had been real once, but the characters who lived them were long ago, and far away. This tale was real, and the one who lived it present, aching with the hurts and triumphs lived just this week.

The banshee thought of the friends she'd laughed with

and loved so long ago; of her own lost mother, who she'd never see again. Tears trickled from her dark eyes, cutting trails down her dirty cheeks.

Angelina looked up and saw the banshee crying just as Warbel swooped low with a glass bottle in his claws. He scooped up the tears, stuffing the cork into the bottle with his beak as he soared away out of the creature's reach.

The banshee screamed with rage. "Thief! You bring those back!"

"She isn't a thief. She's my friend. And you said if I made you cry, I could have the tears. Warbel just collected them for me."

Warbel dropped the bottle of tears into Angelina's satchel and perched next to her horn. "She's right," the wren said. "You never said she had to collect them herself."

"Neither did I say I was bound to let you leave this clearing alive," the hag said. She opened her mouth wide, showing jagged, yellow teeth.

Warbel dove for the satchel, tugging the leather cover over herself. "Cover your ears, child!" she shouted.

Angelina huddled on the ground, clapping her hooves over her ears.

Inhaling deep, the banshee wailed. It started low and deep, but the awful scream built until it shook the fresh green leaves from the trees and made the ground shudder. The swamp water frothed, sending fish and frogs leaping into the air. They landed with ugly splats, floating dead in the stagnant muck. Birds and bugs fell from the trees, their dead eyes staring.

Angelina's heart pounded and her mouth went dry. The terrible wail pounded at her ears, demanding entrance so it could travel to her heart and kill her. But her hooves clapped tight, and the wax held fast, keeping it out.

Warbel huddled inside the pack, the wax in her ears keeping her protected, but the wail made her dizzy and she had to use both wings and claws to steady herself.

Finally, the banshee ran out of breath and stood panting with rage. She glared at Angelina. "You tricked me!" she yelled.

"I did not." Angelina pushed shakily to her feet. "You asked why I was crying, and I told you. It isn't my fault that you have a heart under all that meanness. I'd think you'd be glad of it instead of angry."

"Well, I'm not," the banshee snapped. Then she took a deep breath.

Angelina braced herself, thinking the hag was going to wail again, but she didn't. Instead, the anger faded from her expression, and she smoothed her hands over her ragged dress. She gave Angelina a sidelong look.

"It's true," she said after a moment. "You have beaten me fairly. And to show there are no hard feelings, I have a piece of advice I'll give you for free."

"Don't listen to her, Angelina," Warbel said. "A banshee gives nothing good without cost, and you'd best count your fingers, even when you pay."

"Shut up, you little flying rat!" the Banshee said. Calming herself, she smiled slyly. "It costs me nothing to tell you this. Whatever others may have said, you must trust the wizard. Do whatever he asks of you, or you will never be a human child again. Do you understand?"

Angelina gave no answer. "Thank you for the tears," she replied instead. Spinning on her hind hooves, she ran from the bog as if she was racing for her life.

And perhaps she was.

17: THE WIZARD

The trip back to the wizard's cottage didn't take nearly as long as Angelina thought it would. By late afternoon, she was one turn from the clearing when Warbel landed on a branch next to her.

"I cannot go further with you."

"Why not?" Angelina asked. Then she remembered the wren couldn't go into Queen Felicity's cave either. "Are you and the wizard enemies?"

"Of a sort," Warbel said. "But I will not be far away, and if you need me, I will come, no matter the cost." With that, she flitted up into the trees.

After a moment, Angelina turned and walked into the clearing to find the wizard standing on his front steps, watching for her.

He clapped his hands in delight. "You have returned! And no worse for wear, I see."

Angelina wasn't so sure about that, but she followed him into the cottage, happy for its warmth and comfort after her adventures.

"Did you bring all the ingredients?" the wizard asked.

Angelina nodded absently as she looked around. The

cauldron was far bigger than she remembered, and already bubbling over the fire. "What is for dinner?" she asked, certain that whatever was in the pot, it couldn't contain her potion. There was far too much there for one spell.

The wizard laughed. "Oh, that isn't dinner! That's your cure, my dear."

"Really? I thought you needed the ingredients before you could start."

He waved the suggestion away. "Most spells have a similar base concoction. The binding agents, you know. You've brought the important bits, though. And you got them all." He stroked the satchel still hanging around Angelina's neck. "Oh, very fine. Exceptionally fine, in fact. The queens were always generous, though... to other people, anyway."

He said the last part with such bitterness that Angelina frowned. "What do you mean?"

The wizard twitched as if startled. "What? Oh, nothing, nothing, child. May I have the ingredients?"

Angelina looked at the enormous cauldron, and Queen Aquila's question echoed in her mind. *Why?*

Shrugging off her uneasiness, Angelina ducked her head and allowed him to take the satchel.

The wizard hummed happily and pulled out the first ingredient he touched. "Look at this bottle of wind! How did you capture it?" Angelina told him and he praised her cleverness. "I never would have thought of that," he said. "I probably would have journeyed all the way to Aeolus' island to ask for it."

He set it on the table and lifted out the berries and the sapphire ring, turning them this way and that in the candlelight. "And you say Aquila and Felicity gave you these... freely? All you did was ask?"

"Well, we had a nice long talk," Angelina admitted. "But yes, they did." She blushed but didn't mention the incident with the glowing tiara. There didn't seem to be any point.

He set the five ingredients in a row on the table. "Now, we are ready to begin." The wizard licked his lips and rubbed his hands together.

Dancing and capering, he stirred the pot, pulled a book from a high shelf, and danced some more while muttering to himself all the while.

Angelina looked at the table where dozens of tiny bottles stood empty, as if waiting to be filled. Why would he need so many bottles for a single spell? For one, she could probably drink or use straight from the cauldron?

She glanced into the pot when the wizard wasn't looking. It was full to the brim with bubbling purple liquid. If it was just for her, why was there so much?

Angelina's uneasiness returned. Something wasn't right. Maybe she should call for Warbel? But then she remembered the little wren's words. 'No matter the cost.'

She didn't want Warbel to be harmed, so she waited. She would only call if she truly needed her.

The wizard laughed and sang bits of a song Angelina didn't recognize. The girl-turned-unicorn understood why she should be happy, but why should it matter so much to him? He jumped and clicked his heels together.

So much for being old and unable to travel far, Angelina thought as she watched him. Too many bottles and too much joy. Queen Felicity's voice whispered through her memory. *Why?*

Still dancing, the wizard began dropping the ingredients into the cauldron. As each went in, a puff of smoke drifted upward and he stirred the pot, casting a sly glance over his shoulder at Angelina.

Then he sang the spell.

> *With berries red and jewel of blue*
> *On each new moon, we sing this tune,*
> *With Wind for strength and sun eternal,*
> *Once a month, we drink to the portal,*

To extend this life, and gain full youth
A unicorn's horn will bind our truth.

Angelina turned wide eyes on the wizard. "That doesn't sound right," she said.

The wizard stopped singing and smiled kindly at her. "What part, my dear?"

"The part about the unicorn horn. You didn't tell me you needed my horn."

"Because we already had it," he said reasonably. "Besides, you only need to dip it in the potion when it's done. Nothing more." But he glanced away when he said it and Angelina thought about the rest of the spell.

"That didn't sound like a transformation spell, either."

His eyes narrowed. "Oh? And are you a wizard? What do you know of spellcraft?"

"Enough to know that 'extending life' and 'gaining youth' have nothing to do with changing me back into a human girl."

He blinked. "Is that what I was saying?" He hurried over to the spellbook. "Perhaps I was saying the wrong incantation. I am old, my dear, and occasionally I get confused.

But Angelina was listening to Queen Aurora's voice in her memory. *Why do you trust him?*

"Ah, here it is," the wizard said, and slid his hand under the book. As he turned to face her, Angelina caught the flash of a blade and backed away a step. The wizard came toward her.

Realizing she had seen, he didn't try to hide the knife anymore. "Don't worry. It won't hurt much, I promise."

"You said I only had to dip my horn in the potion. Why do you need a knife?"

"Well, that was for the wrong potion. I just reread the instructions for the correct potion, and—" He jumped at her, and Angelina reared up, lashing out at him with her front hooves. The wizard ducked sideways with a cry.

"Stop it now, you naughty girl!"

"You are the naughty one."

"I'm not," he said pleadingly. "Angelina, don't you want to be human again? I need to cut a bit of your horn for the potion. Then you can drink it and change back into a girl."

"No. All the queens said not to trust you."

"Did they?" His eyes glinted. "Did they actually say, don't trust the wizard?"

"Well, no, but…"

"There, you see? You imagine problems where there are none. Just let me cut a bit of your horn so I can complete the cure. You'll see. It will be fine."

But the glint in his eye and the desperate tremble in his hands worried Angelina. She backed away from the wizard and bumped into a cabinet on the far side of the room. The door came open and something fell out onto the floor. Angelina looked down.

"That's my favorite hair band," she said. "I thought I lost it the day all this started. What is it doing here?"

"Is it?" The wizard inched closer. "I have no idea. I've never seen it before."

But Angelina knew better. She also knew that if a witch or wizard had something that belonged to you, they could cast spells on you and make them stick. She glared at the wizard.

"Yes, it is, and yes, you do. Stay away from me."

"Angelina Belladonna Smith, you are being silly."

But suddenly, all the clues fell into place, and Angelina was through listening to him. "You did this. You turned me into a unicorn."

The wizard laughed nervously. "I did no such thing! Come over here and give me that horn!" He lunged toward her, and Angelina spun on her front feet.

Kicking out with her hind hooves, she connected with a soft thud and the wizard went flying. "That isn't a transformation spell," Angelina said.

The wizard groaned as he pushed to his feet and picked up the knife. "Oh, it is. But once I put the horn in, it won't be the kind you wanted, and it won't be for you."

"Hah!" Angelina said. "I knew it!"

"It won't do you any good. I'm the only one who can lift the curse I put on you, and I won't unless you do as I say. Now let me cut off your horn so I can finish my spell."

"I thought you said you only needed part of it." Angelina eyed the door and backed away as the wizard approached.

"I lied," he sneered. "What else is new?"

"If I give you my horn, will you change me back?"

"No. But if you don't give it to me, I'll have to kill you and then start over with one of your sisters. See this?" He grabbed a book off the shelf and showed her the title. ***101 Uses for Unicorn Horn or Make Your Fortune from the Magical Horn.***

Angelina stared at him in horror.

"You see," he said. "If you take a horn from a real unicorn, they die, and you are cursed for eternity for killing something so pure. But if you change a human into a unicorn, you get all the same benefits, and you can harvest over and over again, because taking the horn doesn't harm the host."

"Why would you do that?" Angelina whispered the question, terrified of the answer.

The wizard stared at her. "I would have thought that was obvious, my dear girl. Money. It does me no good to live forever if I'm poor."

Angelina weighed her options. She couldn't let this monster get her sisters, even if it meant staying a unicorn forever. But she wasn't giving him her horn, either. She eyed the giant cauldron. If he didn't have the potion, he wouldn't need her horn.

The pot was suspended over the fire on a huge cast-iron hook. If she could knock that sideways, the whole thing would fall over, spilling the potion onto the floor.

"Don't even think about it," the wizard said. "I'll just kill you and take your horn anyway. Your middle sister will make a perfectly adequate substitute."

"You are a bad person." Angelina sidled toward the door.

"I prefer to think of it as ambitious. Besides, good and bad are matters of opinion." He held up the knife. "Now, let's get on with this, shall we?"

He lunged for her, and Angelina pretended to run for the door, tricking him into moving away from the cauldron to chase her. At the last moment, she pivoted and ran straight for the fireplace.

"No!" the wizard shrieked. He jumped after her, waving the blade over his head. "Stop!"

Angelina stopped. She put all her weight on her front feet and kicked with her hind legs. She hit the cauldron with one hoof but didn't knock it over. The room vibrated with a monstrous clang and the wizard yelped, diving for Angelina.

He slammed into her hindquarters, sending both of them tumbling sideways into the bulging side of the cauldron. The hook groaned and slid sideways as potion sloshed over the sides of the pot.

"My elixir!" the wizard cried, and he reached to steady the cauldron, but Angelina kicked out again, upending the pot. The unfinished potion poured onto the floor, drenching Angelina completely.

The iron pot clanged to the ground and rolled toward the wizard.

"You wanted my horn," Angelina yelled. "You got it." She poked at the wizard, making him cringe into a ball. Then she tapped the rolling cauldron, changing its direction ever-so-slightly so that it settled over him on its top, trapping the evil little man inside.

Angelina lurched to her feet. She felt funny. Her skin felt all fizzy and strange. She looked down at her hooves and gave a little shriek. They weren't the nice walnut brown they'd been a moment before, but an odd shade of pink. And her fine white coat was... well, still white, sort of, but peachier. Like... her skin used to be before the wizard's curse changed her.

Her head spun, her skin glowed, her legs throbbed weirdly. She stumbled outside and fell to the ground.

"Angelina?" Warbel fluttered down beside her, hopping this way and that, chirping with concern. "Are you all right? You look very strange."

"I feel even stranger. What is happening to me?"

"I think..." The wren hesitated. "I believe you are changing back into a girl."

Angelina looked at her hands, for that is indeed what she had now. Hands and feet, arms and legs, and long, brown hair the color of nutmeg sprinkled with cinnamon.

She was a girl again.

The spinning in her head stopped, and she probed her forehead with all ten fingers. "It's gone," she shouted. "My horn!"

"Well, mostly," Warbel said.

"What do you mean?"

"There's a mirror in the cottage. See for yourself."

Angelina stared at the wizard's cottage. She didn't want to go back in, but something would have to be done about the wizard, so he couldn't hurt anyone else. She rose unsteadily to her feet.

A mighty screech tore the air, and the cottage shot upward on long, yellow legs.

"He must have gotten free of the cauldron," Angelina said.

"Quick," Warbel yelled. "Take the nests before he gets away!"

"How am I going to stop him?"

"Not you. Them!" Warbel yelled.

With a mighty rush of wings, thousands of birds flew out of the trees toward the house.

Finally, Angelina understood. What she thought was a hedge of dried sticks around the base of the house were bird's nests, stolen to weave together into one giant nest. Some strange magic had been used to give the house chicken legs and now, unless they stopped him, the wizard would escape, cottage and all.

Warbel let loose a shrill whistle. "Take back your nests, brothers and sisters. Without them, the legs will not stand."

The birds dove on the cottage and snatched at the sticks, tearing them away from the house in bundles great and small, depending on the size of the bird. Some worked in pairs to take away whole nests, leaving gaping holes in the base of the house.

Shrieks of triumph filled the air until the wizard appeared in the doorway. He swayed with the movement of the house, waving his wand and screaming threats.

"Leave my home alone, you foul winged rodents!" He shot lightning from his wand, trying to drive the birds away, but they dodged his strikes and kept at it.

"He stole their nests long ago, and because of the spell he cast with the nests, the birds haven't been able to make new ones since." Warbel landed on Angelina's shoulder to speak to her. "Now is their chance to take back what he stole from them."

"What about you? Did he steal your nest, too?" Angelina asked.

"Yes. But I cursed him so that he could never leave or move the cottage without all the birds knowing. Once the cottage is in motion, the nests can be taken, so now they can take back what is theirs." Warbel pointed with her beak. "My mate and I were the first to reclaim our nest. He waits in the hawthorn tree for me."

One giant chicken leg slipped free of the house, dissolved into yellow chicken bones as it fell to the ground. A great squawking cry went up from the birds and they renewed their efforts as the house tried to hop away. But the battle was nearly over. In minutes, the second leg dissolved, and bones covered the ground. The birds had retrieved the last nest. They had won.

The cottage crashed to the ground, its white stone walls tumbling over each other; the wizard's books, kitchen tools, furniture, pots, and blankets scattering hither and yon.

The last they saw of him, he was running away, stopping every few yards to look back and shake his fist at them. "I'll get you back. You'll pay for this!"

"You'll leave me and my family alone, Mr. Wizard. Or you'll wish you had!" Angelina called back.

The wizard disappeared into the trees without another word.

EPILOGUE

Hello, still here? I'll bet you want to know what happened to Angelina next, don't you? Well, like all heroines after a glorious adventure, she went home.

Yes, simple as that and very little more.

Warbel guided her through the woods, and they found her mother waiting for Angelina as if she knew she was coming. Mom brushed the hair off Angelina's forehead and traced the star-shaped mark that hadn't been there before — all that was left of Angelina's days as a unicorn. But mom didn't comment, just hugged her daughter and took her home.

The Air Force gave up looking for Angelina after the second day of finding nothing, not even unicorn tracks. They reprimanded the officer in charge of the search for "wasting national resources on fairy tales." His superiors didn't believe him when he said he'd seen the unicorn himself, which just goes to show how foolish superiors can be.

Mrs. Finchhagle still lives two doors down from the Smiths, but they don't pay her much mind. It seems that she sprouted donkey ears the same day Angelina had to run away and only got back to normal when Angelina came home. No one knows how it happened, but Mom grins a funny grin every time they pass her on the street or in the store, and Mrs. Finchhagle never meets Mom's eyes or speaks more than a polite hello.

Mr. Overton won teacher of the year and got a nice prize and a special parking place, too. Angelina thinks it ought to have been more, but Mr. Overton says he's happy with it.

Angelina never heard from the queens again, but perhaps they will show up in other stories, so you'll just have to wait and find out.

Warbel went back to her nest and her mate and when Angelina last saw them, they had three lovely eggs they were tending. Angelina hopes they grow into pretty chicks, which I'm sure they will.

As for Marianna and HollyAnne, they have so far refrained from wishing to be anything other than what they are, but they are getting older, and you never know. If you could wish to be a mythological creature, what would it be?

No, no, I don't expect you to come up with something right away. It is an important decision and bears a bit of thinking about. Meanwhile, I hope you are happy being just who you are, because that is the best creature of all.

THE END
Or is it?

ABOUT THE AUTHORS

Honey and Avery are a grandmother/granddaughter duo who are grateful, each for the other. They share a fondness for cats, chocolate and unicorns. Not necessarily in that order.

Lightning Source UK Ltd.
Milton Keynes UK
UKHW012349231222
414383UK00001B/142